zebratears

T. S. Vallée

CHP Creation House Press

ZEBRA TEARS by T. S. Vallée
Published by Creation House Press (CHP)
Charisma Media/Charisma House Book Group
600 Rinehart Road
Lake Mary, Florida 32746
www.chpmedia.com

This book or parts thereof may not be reproduced in any form, stored in a retrieval system, or transmitted in any form by any means—electronic, mechanical, photocopy, recording, or otherwise—without prior written permission of the publisher, except as provided by United States of America copyright law.

This is a work of fiction. The characters portrayed in this book are fictitious. Otherwise, any resemblance to actual people, whether living or dead, is coincidental.

Select CHP products are available at special quantity discounts for bulk purchase for sales promotions, premiums, fund-raising, and educational needs. For details, write CHP, 600 Rinehart Road, Lake Mary, Florida 32746, or telephone (407) 333-0600.

Scripture quotations marked NLT are from the Holy Bible, New Living Translation, copyright © 1996, 2004, 2007. Used by permission of Tyndale House Publishers, Inc., Wheaton, IL 60189. All rights reserved.

The song lyrics *My Papa* by Maria Lal are used by permission.

Cover design by Nathan Morgan
Map of St. Mary's School: T. S. Vallée

Copyright © 2011 by T. S. Vallée
All rights reserved

Library of Congress Control Number: 2012930750

E-book International Standard Book Number: 978-1-61638-706-8

International Standard Book Number (Paperback): 978-1-61638-877-5

12 13 14 15 16 — 9 8 7 6 5 4 3
Printed in the United States of America

Dedication

I'm so glad I went through what I did, because through forgiveness, I have been redeemed for the damage done to me. God has worked wonders through my broken places and I give Him all the Praise and Glory. I hope my book will help others who have gone through this kind of trauma in the past or are going through it presently, that they too will find hope in forgiveness. Our Lord Jesus is the only one who can redeem and give us peace.

Acknowledgments

I wish to thank my family and friends for their support and encouragement to make this book a reality. I especially wish to thank my Publisher and dear friend Atalie Anderson, for her great advice and professional wisdom that went into the whole process; I couldn't have done it without her.

Hans Unden
Roda Anklesaria
Maria Lal
Becky & Tony Anderson
Nick Anderson
Vicky Anderson
John Unden
Ned & Celesté Clements
Margarita Henry
Marcos Perez
Woodley Auguste
Lynne Lamb
Awilda Aviles-Rivera
Robert Rodriguez
Spring Page
Derrick Gay

The Beach
Chapter 1

The drive to the beach was both thrilling and nostalgic. With the window cracked open I could smell the ocean approaching. My grandchildren, who were preoccupied with their little gadgets called iPods, leaned into me from both sides in the backseat of the SUV, both trying to talk at the same time. My daughter Becky, who was driving, told them to settle down and "stop bothering Nana. We're almost there," but we only giggled, and I hugged them both closer to me.

Victoria, age nine, and Nicholas, ten, couldn't wait to show me the wonders of being at the beach. Vicky grabbed my arm and squeezed it in a hug, saying, "Nana, this is going to be an awesome day," and, "Will you come swimming with me?"

Then Nick piped in with, "Of course she's going swimming, but first we must build a huge sand castle, right Nana?" Nick loved being in charge, while Vicky was a go-with-the-flow type of girl. She was so excited at finally seeing the ocean that I had to keep her in her seat with my hand on her shoulder till we were parked.

"Hurry! Hurry! I want to help pick the perfect spot on the beach," said Vicky while she unbuckled her seatbelt. It was a shame that my son-in-law, Tony, couldn't join us, but serving his country in the National Guard that weekend made me so proud. It is very comforting to know that men like him are out there protecting our freedom. I thank God for blessing me with such a beautiful family.

Ah, the ocean breeze, the soft sand between my toes, and Becky and Nick carrying the cooler to a comfortable spot that was not too close to the water yet out of the main flow of people, cars, and debris tossed about. There wasn't much of a beach left. The sea from past storms that Florida is so famous for had reclaimed a lot of it. I stopped and closed my eyes for a moment to take in the sound of the waves and dug my feet deeper into the cool sand while remembering the beach at which I grew up. I opened my eyes to find Vicky pulling on my arm, jumping in excitement, saying, "Come on, Nana. Let's go! Nick has already started digging, and we don't want him to decide everything about the castle!"

"Great digging, Nick. We will need a few buckets of water to form the sand," I called out. Vicky jumped at the chance to go fill the buckets from the ocean. She made it back with enough water for the job, even having spilled much of it in her rush to get back.

Becky began rubbing some SPF lotion on herself and then tried putting some on the kids' faces and arms as they wriggled and squirmed to get back to their sand sculptures. My arms were covered in sand as our castle took shape. I made a fortress with turrets all around the castle that Nick created, while Vicky adorned it with shells and leaf flags to complete it. Vicky then stood back and gave a shrill cry of excitement, saying, "It's awesome, Nana. Where did you learn to make forts for castles like this?"

"It's a long story, baby," I said. "Someday I will tell you all about it.

"Oh, Nana. Tell me now, please?" she insisted. I looked over at Becky on the blanket, and she put down her book to come over and join us with the castle.

Becky remarked, "Mom, this is great. It looks so real. If there was a sand contest, you three would win for sure."

Nick got up and made a dash to the water to wash off the sand that was clinging to his body, and Becky went with him to make sure he would be OK. Vicky and I just dusted off as much as we could and relaxed under the large umbrella that Becky set up on the blanket, admiring our efforts.

"So, Nana" she started, "how did you learn to make such great forts around castles? When you grew up in India, did you have a beach nearby?"

"Oh, yes, Vicky. I practically lived on the beach, which had a fortress just like the one we built. I was your age at the time," I began to tell her. I could almost imagine myself there at my beloved beach surrounded by the smells, sounds, and people from my past.

"Nana, Nana." I heard Vicky pull me back to reality, her cute face and Shirley Temple curls bouncing around. "Do you want to go swimming first, and then you can tell me all about India and the beach there?" I could see how excited she was to get into the water, so we made a mad dash for the frothing waves.

After a long swim—or, should I say, bobbing with the waves—we all got back to the blanket with a great sense of contentment and now being quite hungry, having worked up an appetite. I helped Becky pass out the sandwiches, fruit, and drinks when I remarked, "I wish this was bhel and a freshly opened coconut!"

They all looked at me like I was crazy. Then Vicky asked, "What is bhel, Nana?"

"Let me tell you about bhel, Vicky. It is the most scrumptious food that was ever created." Nick and Vicky settled between their mother and me and looked up with eager faces for my story. I closed my eyes again and told them that I would take them on a special journey though time. They had to imagine that our beach blanket was a time machine and to hold on tight. They giggled and hung on to my arms and off we went.

Let Us Reminisce
Chapter 2

"Well, kids, first of all let me show you where I was born."

"Are we in India now, Nana?" asked Vicky, to which I replied yes with a nod.

"Go on, Nana," said Nick, showing his sister a scrunched-up nose. "You just have to see where I lived, and I will introduce you to my big sister, Ava."

***

I was born in Bombay, India, to a Polish father and Scottish mother. I lost my father when I was just nine months old. I am told he was a gentle human being who loved science with an open mind. He was also an accomplished artist and interior decorator. He designed furniture and building structures that were considered beyond his time. His beautiful hand-painted murals decorated the walls and ceilings of some beautiful palaces in India. His murals grace the historical section of the Prince of Wales Museum in Bombay, and I only hope they have been preserved for future generations to enjoy. His mark of genius was a treasure to the world and a precious find for me. How I longed to draw, paint, and travel as he did.

My father was also quite fluent in reading and writing nine languages. He was even skilled in Sanskrit, the classical literary language of ancient India, considered by some to be the world's most difficult language. My father had traveled through many countries before reaching India, learning their culture and language, which was displayed in his art. During World War II he was held in a German prisoner of war camp for safekeeping, as his great comprehension of so many tongues made him a valuable asset. To be treated as a spy was truly an unjust reward for such remarkable intellect!

He was released two years prior to my birth. During that time, he continued to paint scenes of life in camp. Even though within the confines of the prison, he found so much of nature to paint in beautiful watercolors. I remember my mother describing his first visit to St. Elizabeth's hospital, where I made my debut. She said he picked up my little hand ever so gently and touched each of my fingers, saying, "Another perfect human being."

I lived at an impressive address called Beach House, which was once a raja's beautiful palace. In its day, when the king lived and ruled there, it stood out like an ornament on a beautiful cake. As you drove up an extensive driveway and you approached the four white marble pillars holding up the second-floor balcony, it gave you a sense of privileged presence. The arches between the pillars had a soft covering of ivy mixed with pink climbing roses that seemed to grow out of thin air. The driveway under the arches served as a drop-off point for people arriving or departing from the palace. Bearers dressed in red turbans and cummerbunds over a white jacket and loose white pants made an impressive statement of elegance while they waited on dignitaries getting in or out of their cars.

You then ascended marble steps onto a multihued mosaic floor. The first door was the main entrance to the palace for government officials, who would gather to discuss the day's agenda. Once in the official part of the palace, you walked into the front foyer, still stepping on a mosaic floor, where murals of beautiful women standing under waterfalls or hunting scenes covered the walls. As you walked into the great hall on your left, chandeliers draped the ceiling and there was a patchwork marble floor of black and white squares under foot. A lavish living room right out of *Arabian Nights* sat in the center of the room on a beautiful fringed carpet. Here, too, there were walls with tapestry and murals that complemented each other. To the far left of the room stood a large polished mahogany table that could easily seat ten. The windows were open, and the sunlight streaked in, making the table shine like glass while the smell of roses from the front garden filled the room.

There was a circular garden at the palace entrance filled with flowers of all varieties amidst a child's dream playground. The garden had a huge sandbox the size of a small pool with a giant slide. At the far side of the garden were two sets of swings that hung from heavy chains. These were not ordinary swings but built for a little prince or princess. The seats were large wooden rectangles, strong enough to hold a child and his/her bodyguard. Next to the entrance of the garden, on the side of the driveway, stood a huge mango tree loaded with fruit ready for the picking. It must have been wonderful to stand on the balcony and just reach across and pick a mango. A staircase reached the balcony from inside the garden so that the royal family could spend leisurely hours looking down on their children at play.

Returning to the inside, the great hall had a short foyer, which also served as a waiting room. It led to the back garden and promenade. You stepped down onto a soft, well-kept grassy lawn, from which you could gaze out onto the promenade and ocean ahead of you. The border of the garden had a three-foot wall lined by a trim hedge with tall palm trees in front of it, spaced at ten-foot intervals. The trees were lit up at night, creating a great compliment to the whole garden. A five-foot-wide pathway of large stonework leading directly to the promenade gave the impression of a giant mosaic floor. Throughout the rest of the garden there were clusters of other flowerbeds neatly groomed in different shapes and sizes, with wrought iron tables and chairs scattered around in shady areas.

The pathway led out onto the promenade, constructed as a fortress with flat areas where one could sit with intermittent square turrets. The promenade served as a secure battlefront. It was encamped on a beautiful beach with a horizon that would astound you. The sunsets were enticing enough to maintain a fixed gaze on the big red ball as it slowly disappeared under the water, for you dared not blink and miss the finale.

The royal family must have walked along the promenade with guards stationed at each turret to protect them while the children raced up and down the long promenade, tiring themselves for a good night's sleep. The public must have walked just below, feeling the soft, cool sand between their toes yet looking up with envy rather than the treasure of freedom under their feet.

This was now a public beach, with people from all occupations taking an evening's leisurely walk. They carried their sandals in hand while holding onto their trouser legs and dodging the frothy waves that reached to grab them. Children flew kites, while the balloon man walked down the beach yelling, "Balloons!" There were also large wheeled stands where peddlers sold everything from pieces of sugar cane to roasted peanuts and especially my favorite snack foods, panipuri and bhel. *Pani* means "water," and *puri* is a deep-fried, salty puffed-up pastry about the size of a ping-pong ball but hollow in the middle. After punching a small hole, you dip it into the pani mixture consisting of water, tamarind juice, hot sauce, finely chopped onions, and coriander. You let the puri fill up with the pani and place the whole ball into your mouth and crunch down. The hot juice flushes down your throat, leaving a wonderful pungent taste, while you chew up the puri, anticipating the next one. The bhel is a mixture of all kinds of nuts and chickpea flavored tidbits, something like nachos with puffed rice, chopped tomatoes, onions, boiled potato bits, green chilies, raw green mangoes, and coriander, covered in a thick sweet-and-sour hot sauce. The sea breeze had a pungent smell of the ocean, yet it carried back whiffs of smoky roasted peanuts served in newspaper cones.

***

"Now can you picture the palace and its surroundings? I just want you all to know, that what I have described is not what greeted me in my life there; it's how I imagined it would have been. We would need to move into the future a bit in our time machine."

However, when growing up there I only remember the garden, with brambles and stumps of what used to be rose bushes. Large cobra holes were now scattered around the yard, and you really had to watch where you stepped. The promenade made a good fortress, but it too had decayed. Part of the wall had cracked and fallen away, while some of the square turrets lost their shape through corrosion and the touch of vandalism. The outer walls seemed to have held up pretty well, even through the battle scars. This was the Beach House of today, but I only choose to remember it completely restored to its full beauty. I missed the beautiful sight watching the sunset over the horizon, knowing that so many sets of eyes over the years had witnessed it too. I remember how I would hold my breath until the sun took its final dip."

"Nana, I just want you to know I am still thinking of bhel. I love nachos," said Nick, "and this bhel sounds like something I would eat." We all laughed watching Nick lick his lips as he stuffed the last of his sandwich into his mouth.

"Someday I will make it for you, but I wouldn't add the hot chilies. I know you love spicy stuff, Nick, but this would be beyond even what you could swallow."

"Do you want me to continue describing the interior of the palace?" I asked.

"It's a little confusing and sad to follow your directions, Nana," said Vicky, "but go back to showing us how it used to be when the raja king lived there. It sounds so beautiful."

"OK," I said with a wink and took them back to the palace in all its grandeur.

***

Back in the great hall, you would turn south and find yourself back in the front foyer, where five other rooms, guest quarters, I believe, lined the long mosaic corridor. At the farthermost end stood the huge palace kitchen and two and a half baths. The other set of wooden double doors at the end of that hallway led to a side entrance of the palace, used only for deliveries and the servants.

"Are you keeping up with me, kids?" I got nods from

all of them, including Becky, who was now into the story too. "Let's go back to the official area at the main entrance to the palace, where another stately staircase with highly polished mahogany banisters leads to the second floor, the royal family residence."

***

These stairs led from the main entrance into a short hallway with double stained-glass doors that opened out onto the large balcony overlooking the front garden. To the left was a great family room, where paintings of the royal family hung, while my father, who was commissioned by the raja, did all the murals up and downstairs. There were scenes of a tiger hunt, and sadly, a beautiful buck with an arrow that had brought it down. These pictures were over trophy cases that held stuffed heads from the raja's kills.

The living room had lazy sunken armchairs arranged in the center of the carpet and divans with long, rolled silk pillows. To the back of the living room were French doors that opened onto a small balcony large enough for two people overlooking the back garden and ocean. I think this balcony was built just for the glorious sunsets! North of the main living room were four bedrooms and a huge bath right out of *Arabian Nights*, while on the south side was a sunken dining room, a moderate kitchen, and two full bathrooms. The back door led you down an iron spiral staircase to the servants' entrance to both floors. The servant quarters were a good distance away from the palace and included a royal laundry and a garage that housed their cars.

Therefore, here is where I was born, but after the fact, with the palace the worse for wear, now converted into rental property by the independent ruling government of India. The ground floor was ours, while another family occupied the second floor.

***

"Now let's meet my sister, Ava."
"What is she to us, Nana? Nick asked, looking a little confused.
"I believe, since she is your mom's aunt, she would be your grandaunt."
"Of course, Nick, she's my grandaunt too!" remarked Vicky.
Becky just shook her head and asked me to continue with the story while memories of Ava and I growing up in boarding school started to flood my mind. "Let's go back in time a little and learn about my big sister."

***

It was decided early in life that my sister, Ava, who was three years my senior, had received our father's gift. After all, she had received personal training by him at the early age of three on how to draw stick figures. He doted on her, while she adored and loved him deeply for the short time he was with us. Ava felt the great loss of her father, so much so that in her innocent mind she believed I was the cause of her sorrow. It appeared to her that I, a baby, had replaced her beloved father. I discovered later in life that my mother would come into my nursery to find me screaming, covered with pinch marks. My mother proceeded to have Ava treated by a child psychiatrist between the age of four and five to help her get over her trauma, while I continued to survive.

My mother, God rest her soul, is a part of my life that

brings memories of unrest and almost unforgivable hard times. She made my youth one of both physical and mental torment. Even my earliest recollections reignite the horror. Once, when I was approximately five years old, she was handed a note by my nanny from my kindergarten teacher implying I had made off with another child's school fees. Without asking me for an explanation or believing her own child would never do such a thing, she grabbed me by my left hand and dragged me into the kitchen, yelling, "Which hand did you steal it with?" all the time holding a fork over a hot gas flame. I cried and tried to explain I had not taken anyone's money, but she did not believe me. The fork was almost red now, and she held my hand and pressed the scorching fork onto it. My skin separated with a hissing sound, and I screamed and tried to jerk away, but the still red-hot fork grazed my right hand, burning a hideous mark to match.

At that moment a calm came over me, and I stopped struggling. I remember it did not seem really to matter anymore. I was looking into her twisted, scowling face, where she seemed to become a total stranger to me. I know I had been marked for life, both physically and emotionally, but at the tender age of five, who knows or understands why a parent would hurt a child? Today I still carry the faded marks on my hands. Of course, she bandaged me up and felt it was a lesson well learned, only to find out the next day from the same teacher that it had been a big mistake. She let my mother know that the money had been found and profusely apologized.

***

"Oh, Nana," said Vicky as she took both my hands and turned them over to see the fork marks. Nick was tracing the marks on my hands, and Becky stifled a sniffle. The marks were slowly disappearing with age, but you could still make them out.

"No big deal," I said. "No need to cry over the past. I forgave her a long time ago, even though she never apologized for judging me that day."

***

She did mention it once when I was all grown up. In her own way she was telling me she was sorry by asking, "You haven't forgotten the fork, Tess, have you?" I told her then that it was forgotten, and I understood that she thought she was doing her best to bring me up decently and honorably, even though the results were hurtful.

Since the death of my father, mother became a homemaker, without a clue at earning a livelihood. She found it necessary to turn our home into a bed and breakfast for reputable bachelors. According to her, that atmosphere was not appropriate for young girls; it was healthier and safer in a boarding school environment in the care of nuns. Mum struggled to make ends meet in a baffled state of affairs, not comprehending how to carry on after years of father's extravagant way of life. He had not made provisions for his family in case of his demise, only to be in debt to bill collectors.

Mr. Singh was one of the first young bachelors to use the now-transformed home. He witnessed her torment and stepped in to help advise her on how to run the place, as well as her finances, thus being able to restore her sanity. I never understood what she must have gone through, only that I thank God that someone was there for her. Little did I know that this was the beginning of the most unsettling and frightening time of my young life.

***

"Let's take a break from these memories, kids. How about a quick swim before we have to head home?" Becky reminded me that we were still in the time machine somewhere in India and had to get back to the present beach in Florida. We had a good laugh and then raced to the water for one more swim. I glanced back at the castle we built, and in my mind I told myself we would return.

As we packed up our time machine blanket, dusted off the sand, and piled into the car. We all sat on towels so as not to mess up the seats. Becky and the kids wanted me to go on with the story, as they were dying to know what happened next. I told them that I would tell them about my first year at boarding school, but they had to promise not to get upset, as it was sad yet quite an adventure.

"OK, Nana, but you have to finish it before we get home, please," Vicky begged.

Nick had an idea. "How about you sleep over, Nana, and we can stay up all night?"

"You mean like a camp out with ghost stories?" I asked. Becky was smiling and had a few memories of her own begin to assemble in her mind. "I know what you are thinking of, Becky. Remember your sleepovers?" Becky replied that she did, and it would be great if we did it with our kids this time. "OK," I said. "It's settled. We are having a sleepover at your house, but someone will have to lend me some pajamas."

    While driving home, I started telling them about my first year in boarding school. Becky turned off the radio so she could hear it too.

Layout of St. Mary's Convent Grounds

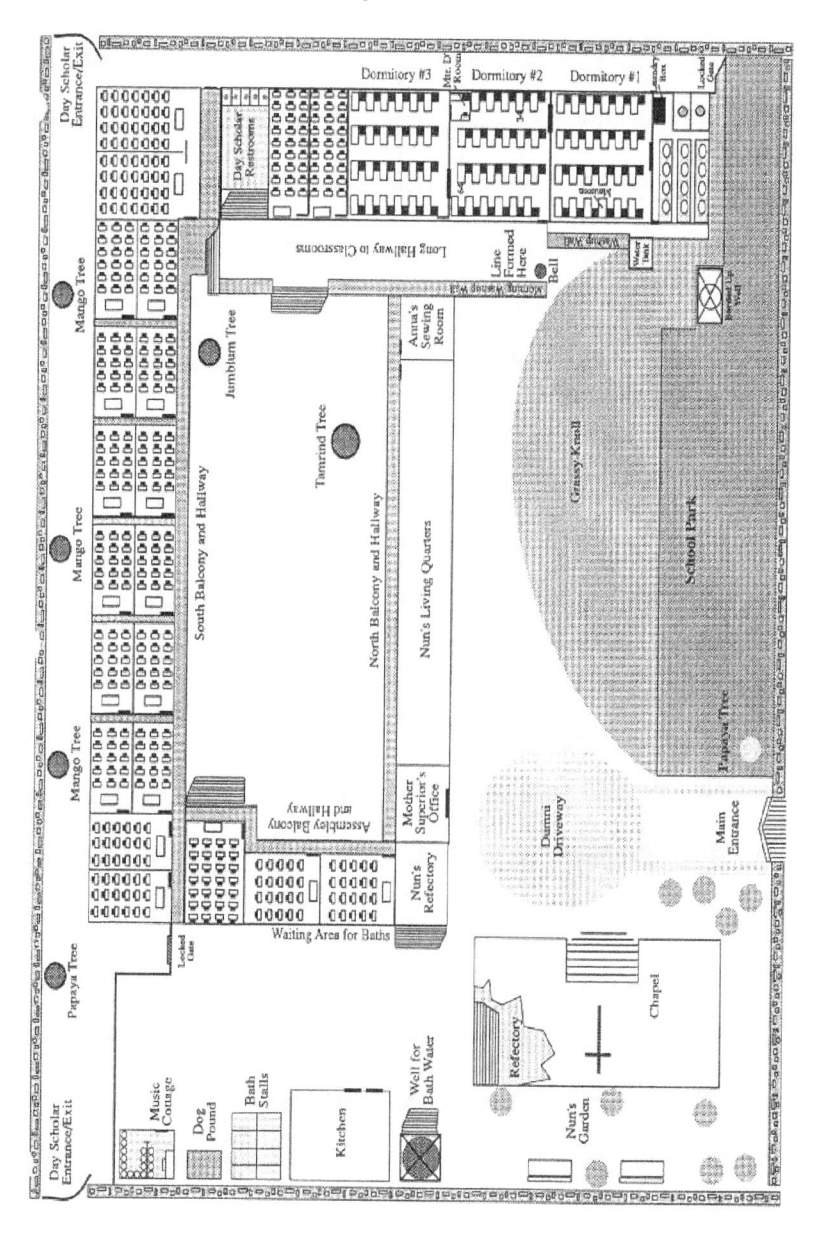

St. Mary's Convent Boarding School
Chapter 3

One of my earliest recollections is when I was nine years old, and I went to join my sister Ava at boarding school. Mum and I traveled overnight by train to get to Belgaum, India.

I took such delight in the train ride, even though the compartment was crowded with so many Indians. The hectic noise of peddlers attempting to sell you their wares at each train stop filled the air. They would literally stick their baskets in the window and run with the train as it took off while trying to retrieve their merchandise. The seats were just planks of hard wood made smooth from constant use, and I found myself moving from one window to another trying to get as much of the sights of the vast but soon disappearing terrain. I stuck my head out of the window, only to have coal dust from the smoke stack hit me in the face. I didn't care though; it was such a new experience that I would break out in songs to the sound of the wheels clanking along. Once it got dark, I must have dozed off, because I heard a commotion of people pulling things down from racks and saw Mummy was busy getting our things together. "Get up, sleepy head," she said. "We have arrived."

Belgaum Station at last! A *coolie* (porter) took Mum's commands on which baggage was ours. They were moving so fast that I had to run alongside just to keep up with them. I was astounded when I saw our taxi, a *dumni* (covered wagon) being led by two oxen. I walked around the whole contraption to make a distinction: Did the oxen have the beefiness to carry my heavy trunk as well as myself? I climbed into the wagon very carefully in order to generate as little weight as necessary for the poor animals, while the driver just hopped on with his whip in hand and made odd clicking noises with his mouth. The oxen seemed to understand him as they pulled out in a slow rumble. The anticipation of getting there the same day diminished, as we traveled at the velocity of a snail.

After what seemed an eternity my body stopped swaying from side to side, which snapped me out of my daydream. We had arrived! In front of us stood a towering stone wall that seemed to stretch as far as the eye could see. Glittering multicolored glass lined the top like candles on a cake, but unsightly barbed wire took away its beauty. I climbed up on the bench to get a better look and behold the gates of heaven, so I thought. Huge iron gates coming together in a pointed arch were held together by a giant chain and padlock. There was a long driveway lined with hedges as tall as the walls, while spider webs as large as four to five feet wide hung from trees that glistened like shiny silken threads in the morning sun. The occupants of the webs were as large as my wide-open hand, which sent adventurous shivers down my back.

At the far end of the driveway, as if in a cluster, I saw the nuns. One of them turned and noticed us there and broke into a run. She reached the gate with smiles and waving, at the same time pulling out a big bunch of keys that attached to her waist. She unlocked the gate and swung them wide open to let the dumni through. I looked back at the gates as we rumbled forward; they were being shut once more, which left me with a foreboding in the pit of my stomach. Mummy seemed preoccupied; she could not have noticed my melancholy face as we reached the end of the driveway.

Mummy looked at me and then out the dumni, not uttering a word. I felt so alone it actually hurt. I started to tell her that my stomach ached but was interrupted by a shout.

"Mummy! Mummy!" Ava was running toward the dumni with flying arms, dressed in white. I wondered then if we were all going to become nuns and have to wear white. Ava's hair shone blackish blue in the sun, yet her cheeks were pale, giving her a stony look. Mummy stepped off the dumni to hug and kiss her. She held her for such a long time, sparking a little envy in me.

I smiled at Ava, and she smiled back, which felt so good. My big sister came up to me, tugged my pigtails, and commented on how much I had grown and how she loved my long hair. My hair was light brown with a dark complexion alongside her snow-white skin. Mummy was now talking with the nuns while I again trailed behind in silence just sneaking peaks at the whole place. She tugged at me to keep up as we entered Mother Superior's office. She introduced me while signing some papers, handing me over to them. I finally got a send-off hug, and Mother Superior instructed Ava to acquaint me with the dormitory so I could settle in. I turned to gesture good-bye to Mummy and saw her face torn with emotions; she had become teary-eyed as she blew us farewell kisses. I ran back to her, gave her a big hug, and told her I wanted to go home, and Ava followed suite. Mother Superior pulled us off her and held onto our arms while she climbed back on to the dumni for her lonely trip back to Bombay.

My trunk was already at the foot of my assigned bed. Ava unlocked it and pulled out my clothes and neatly put them on my bed, remarking, "Your number is thirty-four, and

I'm sixty-four." She proceeded to show me that all my clothes had the number and would explain why at another time. We were to address the nuns by "Mother" and then their name.

Mother Doris, our dormitory nun, walked in at that moment. She looked at me and, without a word, held my shoulders and turned me around, saying, "Welcome to St. Mary's, Tess." I looked up at this towering, dark-faced nun and saw that she wore a smile. Mother Doris picked up one of my socks, noticed the number, and remarked, "Thirty-four. Now I shall remember you." She noticed my puzzled look and waved Ava away as she went on explaining to me. "Tess, come with me, I have to show you around my dormitory and explain the rules. I only do this once, and I expect you to follow them." I felt uneasy and tugged on her long white skirt complaining that my stomach felt queasy. She took me to her room and brought out a bottle and spoon, saying, "Open wide." Yuck, castor oil! I almost heaved on her. I noticed that whenever I was afraid or anxious about something, my stomach would ache, but I learned from that moment on to never complain of a stomachache to her.

She showed me the bathroom, which had about twenty sinks, all lined up and joined in two rows. There was a four-foot-by-four-foot black box with wire mesh on top for our dirty clothes. The Dhobi (laundry person) picked up all the clothes once a week and brought them back folded according to the numbers, which made it an easy method to distribute the clothes on laundry day. The lavatory had two stalls with doors and no commodes. I looked inside and was shocked to see no toilet seat, only a big hole in the concrete platform. I climbed up a step to look in and asked Mother Doris how to use it. She sat on her haunches to demonstrate and then stood up smiling, saying, "You'll get used to it, just like everyone else." There was no toilet paper either, so I inquired. She showed me a stack of newspapers all cut into neat little five-inch squares strung through a wire that hung from the doorknob. I was to take only four pieces with me when I entered the stall, otherwise the container could get too full. The sewage removal was every other day, when someone would come from behind the building and dump the collected waste. She then handed me a basin with my number, thirty-four, in black paint on its side and base and told me to put it under my bed every night filled with water from the tank that sat outside the bathroom. In the morning I was supposed to take it, with toothbrush and towel, just outside the dormitory to a long concrete and stone wall, which served as an open-air restroom, just for the morning ritual of washing up.

There were approximately 150 boarders and only one large restroom. I was yet to discover where we took our baths! There were three dormitories with connecting doors: the first for the very little ones aged two to seven, the middle for children from eight to twelve, while the third one had all the rest, from thirteen to twenty.

By now I was very anxious about remembering all the rules, still clutching my white enamel basin and following Mother Doris all over the place. We had finally returned to my dormitory, and I quickly put the basin under my bed. "Good" she said. "I like girls who learn fast!"

I suddenly heard slamming doors, followed with quite a commotion outside the dormitory. Bursting into the room, a nun whom I had not yet met walked toward us holding a girl by her ear. She was dragging this crying and hysterical child about my age toward Mother Doris, pushing her into her arms. I was stunned! My eyes enlarged as I watched one nun tell the other in hushed tones what the girl had done. Mother Doris took over with the ear and pulled her to her room. I heard the loud sounds of a cane whipping, and I cringed in fear, thinking, "What have I come to?" The silent screams of despair clutched my throat while unnoticed tears welled in my eyes.

I could not tell if I was feeling sorry for her or scared for myself. Maybe it was a bit of both. All I could do was look down at my hands. The memory of scorched fork marks now burned, while my stomach decided to twist in all directions at the same time. I felt doomed! Looking around the dormitory, I tried to find my sister's gaze for support, but she was nowhere around. The room was empty, except for the sounds of whipping and screams. Mother Doris finally came out of her room with the girl, now looking like death warmed over. She limped, with huge, blistering welts on her legs. I watched as Mother Doris made her kneel down in front of her and say, "Thank you for correcting me, Mother. I deserved it." Then the girl got up painfully and limped out of the room.

By now I was cowering in front of my bed wondering what she had done that had been so bad to deserve such a ghastly whipping. Mother Doris walked back to me and carried on talking as though nothing had happened. She saw that I was crying and sternly asked me what was wrong. Between sobs I told her I wanted to go home with Mummy. I got a pat on the shoulder as she laughed and said, "Tess, your mum has given you and Ava into our charge so that you both will grow up to be good Catholic girls. You will not be seeing her for a very long time, so you had better get used to it fast, learn quickly, and stay out of trouble." Just then a bell rang out. I was motioned outside to join the rest of the girls, including Ava, who was telling all her friends about her little sister. When the bell rang we had to all line up in groups of two for the refectory.

What was a refectory? I wondered. What a strange word. We walked in silence because it was one of the rules. The smell that came through the window from the nuns' building was so appetizing that I soon realized we were going to a dining area called a refectory for lunch.

We had turned a corner behind the chapel and started descending some steps. I noticed a huge hall that I assumed was the refectory right under the chapel. The sound of nuns singing came through the ceiling, and we were not to make any noise that could transmit into the church. There were about twenty tables lined up, forming eight rows. The wooden tables and benches seated six girls. I had to wait while everyone else sat at her assigned table. Mother Doris took my hand and led me to a table with an opening. There were shorter tables and benches for the little ones positioned in the center rows, and at the head of the whole refectory was a small desk and chair where Mother Doris sat and read scriptures aloud.

Mother Doris started the prayers and then rang a small bell, giving us permission to eat. We were not permitted to talk, not even a whisper, while we scarfed down the food. I looked at my chipped enamel plate, which had one slice of bread and some brown gravy with a few pieces of potatoes and some peas in it. I had a tin cup with powdered milk in front of me, too, and that was it! I noticed everyone had the same thing, except one section of girls who were eating different food. I started to ask Ava, who also happened to be at my table, why, but the girl next to me nudged me in the ribs. I looked at her, and she put her finger to her mouth to say, "Hush, don't talk!" I nodded in thanks and smiled and proceeded to eat my lunch. Mother Doris was reading aloud, stopping occasionally to sternly look around, determined to catch someone talking. It was quite a harrowing experience for my first of many days, or should I say years, there at St. Mary's.

 I spent the rest of the day making my bed, putting my clothes away, and covering my text books in readiness for school the next day. Ava took me around the school, showing me where the classrooms were and showing me off to some of her friends. Dinner was the same experience, except the gravy had thickened with a few pieces of an unknown meat, and we did get an extra slice of bread. As we ascended the refectory steps, I noticed the sun had set, and we walked in the dark with our path lit by the eerie light from the chapel. We were allowed an hour of play before going to bed. Everyone dispersed and went about with their familiar little groups. There was laughter, some singing, and squeals from the little ones. Mother Doris walked around like a sentry overlooking the play time. I made sure to stay out of her way and found a corner to sit and watch everyone do their thing. Out of almost 150 girls there, I was number 34; I wondered what number 64 was doing.

 I was responsible for one of the little ones who needed extra care. Mina, a four year old, was ordered to report to me that evening, my new little charge. I guess Mother Doris knew I was having a difficult time adjusting to boarding school, so she assigned me to this little one, believing she could take my mind off myself and devote it to focusing on someone else.

Mina seemed shy like me, and yet she was so cute with a few freckles on her nose. She had short brown hair and green eyes. Her skin was almost white, but her features were Asian.

Half hidden behind the pillar I was leaning against, she found me. She poked her head around and smiled, saying, "Mother Doris said your name was Tessa, and I have to listen to you." I smiled back at her and told her to just call me Tess. She jumped up onto the stone wall and sat next to me. So small and cute, her little sandaled feet swung back and forth when she immediately went into her tall tales. I listened with pleasure to her wild imagination, and it was wonderful.

Her favorite story was about a prince who rescued her from a tower infested by big bullfrogs. The prince took a big stick, killed all the frogs, stole her away from the tower, and rode on his beautiful white horse back to his kingdom. Mina was deathly afraid of bullfrogs, which our school had plenty of. She proceeded to tell me that a big black-and-white monster creeps into her dormitory every night and ties a bullfrog to her bed. I laughed and told her that there were no such things as monsters here, and if she ever saw one, she should come and get me. I would protect her!

Mina got quiet, and then slowly turning her head she looked into my eyes with such sadness that it made me sit upright and ask her what was wrong. She put her head down and mumbled, "Mother Doris does tie a frog to my bed because I have a lot of accidents."

"What kind?" I asked, not sure if I understood what

she meant.

Looking me in the face with a horrid scowl she replied, "I wet my bed, that's why!"

I had already accepted that all grown-ups were horrid people, but now I believed they were placed on this earth just to torture little children. I told her that I would help her not to have any more accidents and then the frog would be removed. With a beautiful, big smile, she hugged me, saying I was her new best friend. She took off and joined her other little friends while I sat by myself looking into the night and listening to all the new night sounds of crickets and bullfrogs in the distance.

I wondered what Mummy would be doing at this moment. "She's probably still on the train on her way back to Bombay and our beloved beach home," I imagined. I searched for the sound of the ocean and crashing waves on our promenade, my favorite sounds of home. I remembered how I used to stand at my bedroom window and feel the spray from the ocean waves gently touch my face while I licked the salt off my lips. That's how close we were to the ocean. The waves would smash up against the wall, and the spray would reach the house.

I was so far away in thought I didn't notice Ava and her friends coming toward me. My sister was very popular and had many friends; even Mother Doris seemed to tolerate her. She grabbed my hand and pulled me up to go join her. I was very shy with older kids, and now I was pressurized to join them in the jump rope game. For the lack of companionship at home I had not learned to play many of the games most kids knew. I had not jumped rope before and messed up the game to the point of embarrassment for my sister. Ava could not stand to be ridiculed by her friends concerning her awkward and stupid sister, so she joined in with the others and made me the butt of their jokes.

Finally the bell sounded. Thank God! The girls automatically busied themselves getting ready for the next process. A silence fell over the whole area except for the sound of shuffling feet and directions given by Mother Doris. I followed like a lamb and did what the others did. I picked up my enamel basin and stood in line at the water tank. It was cold, with little bits of rusted metal dropping from the tap and settling on the bottom of my basin. I tried walking very carefully so as not to spill a drop. I placed it under my bed for the morning. Tomorrow would be another very hectic day for me. I was to be fitted for my school uniforms and then introduced to my teachers, and, "Please God, keep me out of trouble!"

Mother Doris had assembled all the girls in their respective dormitories, and everyone was kneeling in front of their beds. I knelt down too, and someone in the third dormitory started the rosary. It was such a long ordeal that my knees hurt on the bare concrete floor. I dared not move, though, as I felt the glare of Mother Doris on my neck. When it was finally over the lights were to go out in five minutes. Ava came over and showed me how to install my mosquito net and how I was to fold and put it away every morning under the mattress. It tied to track wires that ran from one end of the dormitory to the other by four-cornered string. When let down it had a slit on the side you entered your bed. Ava began to tuck it around the mattress, and I was to fold the opening over and tuck it in from the inside.

Once I lay down and settled in for the night, Ava

stuck her head into my mosquito net and looked me straight in the eye. She opened her mouth to say something then changed her mind. She smiled at me and said, "Good night." Just her smile made me feel so good that it made it all right to be there. I retucked the opening and closed my eyes.

I awoke suddenly to a loud scream. I was not sure I had really heard it or just dreamed it. I dared not get out of bed, or Mother Doris would surely punish me. I could not go back to sleep either, even though I kept my eyes closed. I heard Mother Doris walking past my bed and later discovered that she walked for an hour around the dormitory with a long, thin cane in her hand to make sure no one was awake and talking.

It must have been much later that night I heard the loud screams again. I sat upright in bed trying to see in the dark through my mosquito net when I heard someone running in the direction of the first dormitory. I climbed out of bed and followed her flashlight that danced off the walls. I peeked through the open door and saw Mother Doris grab Mina and yank her out of bed, slapping her around the head telling her to be quiet. She now pulled her sheets off the bed and draped them over Mina's shoulders, making her kneel in front of her bed. In the quick movements of her flashlight, I could see shadows of a bullfrog jumping madly around poor Mina. She was hysterical and yet suppressing her screams from being beaten by this huge monster in white! My heart went out to her. I wanted to run in there and kill the white monster. My feet felt like lead though, and even when the monster turned to walk back, I could not move. I was frozen with fear; Mother Doris was right in front of me, looking down into my terrorized face while shining the flashlight right into my eyes.

Her hand outstretched, she pointed toward my bed. Since I could not will myself to move, she nudged me in that direction. I walked in silence, forcing my feet to move and grateful that I was finally within my safe zone, my bed. I started to climb in when she decided to speak. "Come with me, Tess," she said in a very kind voice, engulfing me into a false sense of security. I guess I needed it to take the next move in following her. She closed the door and turned on the light. I was now looking at her in a long white nightgown with her hood off. She wore a white night cap of sorts, covering her almost baldhead.

She had a very simple room: a crucifix hung at the head of the bed, a desk, and a sunken cupboard on the wall near the door. She sat down at her desk and pulled me closer to her. With a quiet and almost human voice, she asked, "Why did you leave your bed?" I told her I had heard screams and wondered what had happened. I had broken her rules, she informed me, and that would have meant a severe punishment, but since it was my first night there she would let it pass. I was never to leave my bed again at night under any circumstances, unless it was for the sole purpose of using the bathroom.

I nodded in agreement and hoped to get back to my bed, expecting the reprimand was over. I backed off a little bit when she raised her pointy finger at me, saying, "Remember, Tess, Mina is your responsibility from now on, and you had better make sure she uses the bathroom before going to bed." I found the courage to ask her if Mina was sick, when she shook my shoulders so hard that hearing what she said came out in spurts. I was never to question her authority again, or I would face the consequences. Still shaking, I left her room, made a mad dash for my bed, and crawled under my sheet, trying to blot out the memory. I calmed down a bit and vowed I would try to help Mina from now on, and may God help me!

It seemed I had only just closed my eyes when the bell rang. I wondered who was in trouble now. I looked at the barred windows and saw that it was still dark outside, yet everyone was getting out of bed, wrapping up their mosquito nets and putting them away. They looked like a sleepy group of zombies all doing the same thing. They bent down and picked up their basins with a towel on their arm and soap dish with toothbrush secured in an awkward grasp. I watched them until I found myself doing the same. The moon and stars were still out; it was five in the morning. I was learning hourly, then daily, all the rules and routines that were to take place from then on.

It was 5:30 a.m., and we lined up at the sound of the bell. We were going to morning mass in the chapel over our refectory. My stomach growled with hunger while we climbed the steps to church. How I wished we were going in the other direction so we could have breakfast instead.

I climbed the steps and entered a beautiful chapel. It was illuminated in a soft glow by candles everywhere, while music from the organ flowed down as if from heaven itself. I looked around and noticed the choir loft and all the rows of pews in the back filled with nuns dressed in white and kneeling in prayer. It was like looking out at the ocean, their heads bobbing in prayer, making it look like the white froth of the waves. Mother Doris's eyes caught mine and with a stern look pointed my gaze to the front.

It had been so long since I attended mass, and I thought it would be wonderful to receive Jesus into my heart again. I had so much to tell Him that I felt I could only really make contact through Holy Communion, while He was still in my mouth. "I have You now, Jesus," I told Him as I knelt in my pew with Him on my tongue. He was so small and delicate that I did not want to bite down on Him in case I hurt Him. I closed my eyes and imagined myself in my own mouth, sitting on my back molar, with Jesus sitting right next to me. I felt quite shy but comfortable enough when talking to Him.

Jesus had on a long, white robe with beautiful, flowing brown hair that rested on His shoulders and the most wonderful eyes, which could see right through me. He smiled and told me how good it was to see me again and that He was happy I had come to visit. Jesus and I were the same size to be able to fit in my mouth, about a quarter-inch tall. He seemed to know what was troubling me and how I wished I could stay with Him always, never having Him leave me. I heard Him tell me that He loved me so much and that I could talk to Him whenever I wanted, not just in church. I asked Him if I could talk to Him while in school or lying in bed or even while eating. He smiled and nodded, saying, "Anywhere and anytime, Tess."

I felt a nudge on my arm. It was like an earthquake inside my mouth, making me lose my balance. Jesus grabbed me before I fell and held me close to His chest.

I opened my eyes and saw one of the girls trying to tell me to get off my knees and sit down like the rest of them. The priest was giving a sermon, and I was distracting them by staying in the kneeling position. I hated to say good bye to Jesus, but I had to move. I sat down but still had the now-soggy Communion host on my tongue. I smiled to myself and told Jesus to be careful going down and to bless all the parts of my body as He passed them to my heart. I pictured Him passing my ribs as if riding on a long slide. My stomach growled, and I thought how loud that must have sounded to Him. It was such a wonderful feeling knowing that I had a special friend I could talk to anytime.

We grouped into a line right after church and walked down to the refectory. To my dismay, breakfast was a repeat of dinner with an exception of tea instead of milk. I was so hungry that I did not care about etiquette. I dipped my slice of bread in the tea and ate the gravy with a spoon as though it were soup. I found myself staring at the table with the girls that had such a variety of food. I gave Ava a questioning look, and she whispered, "Rich girls," and kept eating. I couldn't help staring at them eating eggs, bacon, and toast with large glasses of milk. They didn't have tin cups or enamel plates but fine china. How lucky they were that I was at a safe distance, or I would have grabbed their food at the risk of punishment.

Ava later explained about the rich girls whose parents were people in high governmental positions paying an exuberant price for their schooling. They received care packages almost every other week with supplies and snacks.

The sunken cupboard in Mother Doris's room was standing open now, displaying all kinds of wonderful treats of candy, bubble gum, and cookies. Each container had the rich girl's number on it, and she was allowed to pick one or two items for the day. With my eyes focused on the life of the rich and famous, I could still hear Ava telling me that we were charity cases, as all our mum could afford was the school fees. We were to be very grateful that we received our uniforms and food free. I walked back to my bed and locker and started tidying up for inspection. Mother Doris was due to walk along each row of beds and open lockers while we waited for her approval before leaving for school.

***

I found Vicky and Nick clinging to each side of my arms with huge sighs as though they had held their breath all through the story. Vicky began by patting my hand and saying, "Oh, Nana, how awful. Was Mina OK, and did you get rid of the frogs?"

"Not right away, Vicky, but I did help her have fewer accidents, which meant less time spent with them."

Nick hugged me closer and remarked, "You were so brave, Nana. This is turning into quite an adventure. I really don't like that Mother Doris. She sounds so evil."

"Well, we are almost home," said Becky, "so let's wait till we are inside and cleaned up before we continue."

"Nana!" yelled Vicky from the bathroom later that night. "Don't start without me!" I went up to the bathroom door and told her that the story would wait till we are all back in the living room, cleaned up, and in pajamas. Becky, in the meantime, stuck a pizza into the oven for dinner and organized some bean bags in front of the couch. It looked like we were in for a long night of adventure.

Now that we were all gathered in the living room with dinner out of the way, the kids had their pillows to snuggle with while sinking into their bean bags. Becky sat next to me on the couch. I then explained, "We are going to meet a real guardian angel named Anna, and I know you will all love her as much as I do."

    Nick wondered if I could see the angel, or was it a spirit, like a ghost? "No, no, she was a real person," I said. "Is everyone ready to hear about Anna?" I got some enthusiastic nods, so I continued.

Discovering Anna
Chapter 4

The din outside the dormitory increased as the day scholars started arriving. They did not have to talk in hushed tones since they were not under the same rules as the boarders. I had no uniform for my first day of school, so Mother Doris handed me to another nun, who escorted me to the uniform room. A woman about forty years old sat at her sewing machine pumping the iron peddles, not looking up to see us enter. I realized then that the convent had other people working there, not just nuns. She finally stopped and glanced over her glasses, sizing me up for a fit. She got up, went into another room, and came back with a navy blue pinafore with wide pleats that went from below the square neckline to the hem. It had a light blue sash for a belt and a white short-sleeved blouse. I was told to put it on while she pinched the waist here and there. She felt the length past my knees, almost to my ankles, and said, "Perfect fit."

    I looked at her and frowned, because I felt like a lost potato in a very large empty sack, and I told her so. The nun lovingly tapped me on the head and smiled, saying, "It's only for today, Tess. Anna will sew you a set of uniforms. Come back here after school to pick them up, understand?" I nodded and walked away with the nun as I tightened the sash to raise the uniform length, all the while still looking back at Anna with pleading eyes to get her attention and ask her to do better with my uniforms. Anna resumed her sewing but looked up over her glasses at me with a smirk.

    After the main assembly, first period was always religion taught by Mother Clara. She was a short, thin nun with very dark skin. When she smiled, her eyes and teeth shone so bright. She took me by the hand and brought me to the front of the class while the other nun who had escorted me there waved to everyone and left.

    Mother Clara looked at a folder that was probably mine and then smiled. She introduced me to a sea of faces I did not know yet. "This is Tess, and she has come all the way from Bombay as a new boarder, and I want everyone to welcome her. I will also want one volunteer to take her to her next class," and before she could finish her request, a mighty wave of hands raised to volunteer for the task. I was so thrilled to see that they all wanted to be my friend, and I could not wait to discover who they all were. We were into our catechism book going over the prayers we needed to learn by heart when the bell finally sounded and my classmates escorted me two doors down to the next room.

    This was Miss Vosanty, an Indian woman wearing a sari. She was very pretty, wearing a white, tight blouse under her sari made of a beautiful silky blue material that repeatedly wrapped around her waist and ended casually thrown over her left shoulder. "Welcome, Tess. I am Miss Vosanty, your Hindi teacher. Do you speak Hindi?" I explained that I had not yet mastered the art of conversation. She laughingly remarked that I would be speaking Hindi like a "pukka Indian." I guessed *pukka* meant "perfect" or something! When the bell rang, everyone left the class and went back to the main classroom to retrieve their lunch pails. They moved out to the hallway and opened up their lunch pails to eat. The smell that filled my nostrils was enough to make me faint. I took long whiffs as I slowly walked toward the door.

    Ava found me through the crowds of girls and

grabbed me by the arm. "Let's go. Everyone is waiting in line for lunch. You can't waste time standing around and talking, or you will be punished without lunch." I was so embarrassed when the day scholars heard her say that. I wanted the ground to open and swallow me up. I could see their puzzled faces while she pulled me away from them. I began to run alongside her as she held on to my wrist. We finally caught up to the line that was walking away. We were the last two in line, and I could see Mother Doris's angry face as she stopped walking, waiting for us to pass her. She resumed walking next to me, saying that this would be the only time I could be late. "In the future don't bother coming to the refectory if the others have left," she said sternly.

Lunch consisted of a little rice and, yes, the same gravy. This time there were bits and pieces of boiled eggs mixed in. The girls called it "egg curry." I was still hungry after leaving the refectory when I asked Ava, "What now?" She shrugged her shoulders, telling me to go find my new day scholar friends, as they could tell me which would be my next class after lunch. I agreed and took off in a run.

There they were, sitting on the concrete floor in the hallway. Some were skipping rope, while others were playing stone jacks and yet others were still eating. The day scholars had brought lunch from home in little round tin containers that stacked one on top of the other, which separated the different foods. A metal band held it together from the base up, and it locked when you turned a small handle. These containers are dabbas, an Indian-style tiffin box. The girls all picked and shared from each other, a buffet served for a queen. Their food smelled so wonderful that my mouth watered for a taste.

One of the girls, Philomena, I think, nudged me to try some, so without hesitation, I got on my knees and reached for a roti (flat bread). With my fingers I picked up a chunk of meat, some curried vegetables, and Indian salad. I filled my roti with all the ingredients and rolled it up like a burrito, and with a couple of bites I had consumed the whole thing, dripping curry sauce all over the front of my uniform. "Oh God, how wonderful was the taste," I told them. The girls started giggling, because they thought they had never seen a white girl enjoy Indian food so much. *I wish I could do this every day*, I thought. *Missing the refectory for lunch wouldn't be so bad.*

The girls had fun fixing me different variations of filled roti and watching me devour the food. They invited me every afternoon to help them finish their lunches if I wanted. I confided in them that we did not get too much to eat as a boarder and would appreciate anything they had to spare. Of course, Mother Doris would never hear it from my lips, and I hoped there were no boarders watching me stuff my face with such delicious cuisine. From then on every lunch during the week became a banquet for me. The girls turned into such good friends and enjoyed bringing in different foods for me to taste. They would add hot chilies just to see if I could do it. They just couldn't believe I could eat such spicy, hot food and thought they had created a spice monster.

School let out that first day at 5:00 p.m., when the day scholars went home and the silence within the confines of the school was deafening! Anna was waiting for me with my new uniforms, but when I entered the room she had this look of disbelief on her face. "How could anyone destroy a uniform in one day?" she yelled. My smile left my face immediately, as I looked down my dress.

"Oops!" I was such a terrible mess. I wouldn't have to tell anyone of my dining experiences; they could see it all over my clothes. I tried brushing off all the dried-up curry stains from the uniform, but to no avail. She came around her sewing machine with her hands raised and brought them down on my shoulders. I got a good shaking, with a couple of slaps to my head, and then she literally ripped the uniform off me. She left me standing in my petticoat and white blouse while she immediately soaked it in a sink that was in the corner of her room. I was crying now, as I heard her say, "Mother Doris will hear of this."

I begged Anna, "Please don't tell. I am so sorry, Anna." I promised I would do anything for her if she would just forgive me. I even hugged her while she pried my arms off her waist, telling me to take my new uniforms and leave. I slowly walked out of the room, carrying my uniforms as though they were made of gold, and then I heard her say, "You come back tomorrow after school and help me sweep the room, and I won't tell." I ran back to her and hugged her again, and this time she smiled and returned my hug.

By now I was considered old news around school and had conformed to its rules and regulations, although I enjoyed some good lunches now and then when the opportunity arose. I visited Anna more often after school, which was the best thing that could have happened to me. Anna became my best friend, to whom I could pour my heart out. She kept all our talks confidential, and I found her to be a great counselor. When I found out that we took a bath only once every two weeks, Anna would sneak me into the bath stall once a week with water she pulled up from the well. We didn't have hot or cold running water for baths; instead we physically pulled a bucket from the well. It was always cold, but Anna would say it was for her, and the kitchen worker would allow her a bucket of hot water to mix. Anna would get into one stall and wait until I had finished my bath, and I would always leave enough water for her to wet her hair. I would sneak back to the dormitory while she walked back into the kitchen with the empty buckets and her hair tied up in a towel.

To describe the place as sanitary would be an overstatement; it consisted of eight bath stalls with four metal walls and a tin roof. While pouring water from the bucket over your head, you stood on a four-foot square flat, smooth stone placed on the ground. The bucket didn't hold too much water, so we had to be conservative with its use. In addition, a broken wooden chair held your clean clothes and towel. It was always a struggle to try and not wet the clean clothes by keeping them far enough, but there was the dilemma of having to walk onto dirt after a bath to reach the clean clothes. What is a girl to do?

All the bath stalls connected to each other and stood outdoors, detached from the school building but close enough to the kitchen. Just past the bath stalls stood a dog pound that held two of the most vicious German shepherd guard dogs. On bath day, we would line up against the school wall waiting our turn at a bath. This was the only day we could groom our hair with trims, cut our nails, and be treated for lice. It was a noisy two-hour wait with everyone talking above the sound of barking dogs, but for a time of freedom from Mother Doris's clutches it was well worth it.

My first letter-writing day was quite an experience.

Once a month, we had to write letters home. We received letters regularly from Mummy, addressed to both of us, and so we took turns reading them. Her letters always said the same things, encouragement to do well in school and to behave ourselves for the wonderful nuns at the convent. Writing back to her probably had the same effect, as we were not permitted to write what we wanted, thought, or felt.

With one piece of paper and ten minutes to finish, I poured my heart out to Mummy telling her how I hated it there and wanted to come home. I asked for another sheet of paper, as front and back could not contain all I had to say. When I approached the desk, Mother Doris looked up from the book she was reading and asked if I was finished writing. When I asked for more paper, she put out her hand for my letter and proceeded to read it. Her face had a sadistic smile while she ripped it into small pieces and handed me another piece of paper saying, "Write a better letter."

I didn't understand what she meant and started to write all I had written before, properly checking for grammar and spelling mistakes. I found I was the last one remaining while all the others had finished and left the room. Mother Doris came and stood behind my desk looking over my shoulder. She reached down and put a blank page in front of me, removing the one I was writing. She laid the whole stack of letters written by the others next to my page and told me to read a few. I gave her a puzzled look, and all she did was point to the stack of letters. I looked back at them, read the first one, the second, and then the third, and realized they were all identical. I looked at her and saw her smile. "I want you to write a letter just like those," she said while ripping up my second letter. This is what I recollect I wrote, "Dear

Mummy, I am doing well in school, and I love it here. The food is great, and I am studying very hard. Love, Tess."

After that lesson in letter writing, I always sat next to Ava and copied off her page, just adding my needs and wants at the end of each letter; at least it sounded a little different. There were times I would just sign next to Ava's signature and be done with it.

Almost a year later I asked Mother Doris on letter day if I could ask my mum for a parcel since it was going to be my tenth birthday soon. She nodded her approval, and I was allowed two sheets of paper to fill in my request. I asked Mummy to please send me a birthday dress with new shoes, the shiny black ones; lots of bubble gum; a cake with candles; and anything else she wanted. I wanted so much to receive a parcel from home as the rich girls did and maybe get a place in the cupboard with my number thirty-four on the jar.

I was almost ten years old and had never tasted bubble gum. I remember on one occasion Mina came, took me by the hand, and wanted me to follow her. She said she had something great to show me. The rich girls hung out by themselves, never socializing with the rest of the riff raff. From a secured place behind a pillar we watched the wonders of bubble blowing. I could not believe how they blew such huge bubbles without hurting themselves.

After watching them for a while, Mina pulled me aside and opened her hand. She held a big wad of bubble gum rolled up into a pink ball. She had the cutest smile as she tried dividing it, then popping her half into her mouth. She started chewing and tried to blow bubbles as the other girls did but had not quite mastered it. I still held the piece she gave me and wondered where she had gotten it. She laughed, giggled, and said she had picked it up after the girls had thrown it away. She did say she had washed it good and that we should follow them to see where they would throw their new batch, as it would still taste sweet. Wow! I thought, for a four year old, she was so bright; because the new batch was still sweet even after rinsing thoroughly. Mina and I spent many a playtime practicing blowing bubbles. We had a secret place behind the water tank where no one could see us, not even Mother Doris. Now I wanted to taste bubblegum from the beginning, fresh out of its wrapper.

I waited so patiently for Mummy's parcel to arrive in time for my birthday. Every day after school I would run to see Mother Doris and ask if it had arrived, and every day she shook her head no. September 24 was here, and there was nothing yet in the form of a parcel.

I went to sleep that night feeling very sad and disappointed. I awoke once that night to use the restroom, and on my way there I awakened Mina. Her bed was still dry, and I figured I might as well take her along, hoping to avoid an accident. Mina was getting a lot better at not wetting her bed, and the frog no longer scared her. I would pet and play with it, showing that it could not hurt her.

It was 5:00 a.m., time to get ready for mass. I stepped out of my mosquito net and got the shock of my life. At the foot of my bed was a straight-back chair covered with wonderful things. There was a beautiful new frock and shiny black shoes, even a new pair of socks. The dress was light green with little yellow ducks. It had puffed sleeves and three layers for the skirt. It was the most beautiful dress in the whole world. Ava came around with a big smile, and so did Mother Doris. I could not believe that Mother Doris could even smile. She said I could wear the dress for my birthday all day so everyone would know it was my special day. I jumped up and down and tried to hug her, but she pushed me away, telling me to hurry up.

    I rushed around with my basin and washed up. I stood there just staring in disbelief. Ava, being such a great artist, had made a colorful sign saying "Happy Birthday, Tess" taped to the back of the chair. My dress with all its frills sat on the chair with the shoes and socks just poking out from under it. There was a large wrapped box on the floor under the chair with a card. "That will have to wait until after school," Mother Doris informed me, as she started shooing all the girls away from me to line up for mass.

    I felt like a princess as I walked in line to mass that morning. I found a place to sit next to Anna. She looked so happy to see me that morning, pinching my arm gently to wish me my happy day. I leaned against her, letting her know I loved her for making me such a beautiful dress, even if mummy had paid for it. Anna had chosen the colors and designed the dress; she had even gone to the store outside our school for my shoes and socks, doing this just for me!

    When Jesus came to visit that morning, I danced on my molar for Him. I held my new dress on each side and turned around asking Him, "How do I look?" Jesus just laughed and hugged me. I felt so happy to be alive and have the love of two of the most wonderful people in the world. I told Jesus how nice Anna was and wondered if He had met her. I pointed to my right and asked Him if He could see her through my mouth. I told Him to please watch over my friend and make sure that Mother Doris never finds out about her kindness toward me. Jesus put His finger to his lips and smiled. I waved good-bye to Him while He slid down my throat, and I opened my eyes to see Anna on her knees too, her hands clutched in prayer.

At school assembly that morning I felt so distinct. I was the only one in a pretty dress, while everyone else, even the rich girls, had on their school uniforms. My classes were so exciting that day, because everyone treated me so special, touching my dress and the silky white ribbons that tied my pigtails. I could have floated on air all day, not wanting it to end. I especially enjoyed the lunch that my friends shared with me, taking extra care not to drop anything on my new dress.

After school I visited Anna to thank her again for my beautiful dress and tell her about my day, but she wasn't there. I was looking all over for her when I bumped into a nun coming into the room as I was leaving. It was Mother Virginia, my piano teacher. "Where is Anna, Mother?" I inquired. She told me that Anna had to leave the school for a few days because her mother was very sick and needing her care. I got so upset that she wasn't there, because I needed to tell her about the wonderful day I had.

I went back to my dormitory and found the big box sitting on my bed. I sat down and dropped the card on my pillow and began opening the present very slowly, wishing Anna could have been there to see what I had received from Mummy.

Ava and a bunch of girls stood around my bed while I opened up the box. It was full of wonderful surprises. It was not just one present but many little ones: notebooks, pencils, a sharpener, a small paint box, a big bag of bubble gum with other mixed candies, six handkerchiefs with my initials and number, and best of all, a holy picture of a beautiful angel holding the hand of a little girl while she crossed a dangerous-looking bridge. I turned it over, and there it said, "My dearest Tess, Have a happy birthday, with God's blessings. Your friend always, Anna." I pressed the picture to my heart and noticed the girls picking up and looking over all the gifts inside the box. I wondered how Anna's present got inside a parcel from Mummy.

    I pulled Ava aside and showed her my beautiful picture. That was when I learned that Mummy could not send me a parcel because it was too costly. Mother Superior received some money from her to buy me a dress and shoes. However, where had all the presents come from? Ava said that Anna had arranged for all the rest. That meant that all the presents were from Anna and not Mummy! I picked up the card and opened it. Ten rupees lay in it with "Happy birthday, darling. Your ever-loving Mums." I suddenly felt quite angry that the parcel had not come from Mummy, only the card and money. I was sadder yet that Anna wasn't around for me to thank her. I really needed her hugs right then. I tried to understand what was happening to me, but my mixed emotions only brought on a burst of tears. Only Mina stayed at my side, while the others disappeared. I guess no one understood how I felt. How could they?

    Mother Doris came to my bed and told Mina to leave us. She started gathering up all my goodies and dumped them back into the box. She picked up everything, including my card and picture from Anna and asked me to follow her to her room. Once there Mother Doris dumped the box onto her bed. "What's this for?" she asked, picking up the two notebooks.

"I guess for writing stories. You know how I like to write," I cried. She put them down while handing me my new handkerchiefs. She picked up the candy and bubble gum and asked if I wanted to put it in her cupboard, and I nodded yes. Nevertheless, as she started to unlock the cupboard, I got to thinking that it wasn't nice to keep it all to myself; there were so many girls that didn't have any candy. Anna would have wanted me to share it with everyone. I told Mother Doris that I wanted to give it all out to the girls and only keep the bubble gum and cookies in a can to share with Ava and Mina. She nodded and gave me the huge bag of candy to hand out at dinner that night. I took a handful of bubble gum and put them in my pocket, realizing that I didn't have to save the used ones stuck under my bed anymore. I was again temporarily happy, and I could not wait to tell Mina to get rid of her old gum too and to make room for new ones! Mother Doris opened my card from Mummy, saw the ten rupees, and looked at me with a questioning look. I told her I wanted to give that to Anna for making me my beautiful dress, and she agreed.

    Mother Doris handed me a new pencil, eraser, and the sharpener and put the rest of them away in her desk to hold for me. I picked up the bag of candy with the rest of my gifts, especially the picture from Anna, and stuck the ten rupees in my pocket for her. Mina had snuck back into my dormitory and was sitting on my bed, kicking her legs back and forth waiting for me. When she saw Mother Doris and me come out of the room, she jumped to her feet and started straightening my bed. I smiled and grabbed her by the hand, opening her tiny fist, and put a brand new piece of Bazooka bubble gum into it, still in its original wrapper. She opened her hand and squealed with joy. I told her not to open it yet, that we would go outside and find our secret bubble gum spot to experience the opening ceremony together. She stuck her gum into her pocket and waited for me to put my things away. I gave Ava a handful of candy and a few pieces of gum too, and she took off to play with her friends.

    Here we were at last! Mina and I sat on the grass behind the water tank where no one would ever bother us because of the mosquitoes. We carefully opened our gum and found it came wrapped in comics. I read it to Mina, but somehow we didn't understand the joke. Now we were ready for the treat and finally popped the gum into our mouths. It was hard as a rock but oh so sweet. We closed our eyes and relished the wonderful taste that we had only imagined for so long. We did have a couple of accidents in swallowing the whole piece before it got a chance to change from sugar to gum; this meant a couple more new pieces before we mastered the chewing. Between slapping mosquitoes off each other, we started blowing bubbles, small ones, and then big ones that covered my nose when it popped. Mina had still not been able to blow a big one and had fun just poking her finger into the big ones I blew.

    The bell sounded, and it was time for the dinner line. We jumped up and ran toward the dormitory so I could retrieve the bag of candy to hand out. Mina and I were partners in line, while Mother Doris walked behind us. She made her spit her gum out and then sent her running to catch up with me. I smiled at her and touched my pocket, reassuring her that she could have more at playtime tonight.

***

It was really late, and I noticed that both Nick and Vicky looked like they were really trying hard to stay awake. I looked at Becky and asked if we could continue tomorrow, as the next adventure was too good to miss on sleepy kids.

"Let's go to bed, you two," said Becky while the kids climbed out of their bean bags to hug me good night.

"Remember, Nana," said Vicky, "we want to hear all about it tomorrow, right after breakfast OK?"

"I'm so glad you had Anna in that horrid place. You must be so brave!" said a very sleepy Nick.

"I couldn't have made it without her. That's why I believe Jesus sent her as my guardian angel. Good night, my darlings, and I'll see you in the morning."

After they left, I told Becky that there is a part in my story that was not suitable for their young ears. "I will tell you about it when we stop for another break in my story." She looked concerned but understood. "I will have to stop the story after the next adventure when Ava and I go home for Christmas. After all, it will be just in time to end the sleep over and promise to continue at another time."

I slept so soundly that I didn't notice Vicky and Nick had snuggled up against me on the couch watching their cartoons with the volume turned down to minimum. When I started stirring they both jumped up and wished me a good morning and wanted to know when we could get started again on the rest of the story. "We will have to wait till your mom wakes and we have breakfast," I said, so they ran to Becky's room to wake her.

"Let her sleep," I called out, but I was too late. I went into her room to see the kids rolling in her big bed and trying to coax her to get up.

The weekend was passing so quickly, and Tony would be home that morning from the National Guard; I was sure very tired and needing a rest. I got up, got ready for breakfast, and packed my little bag and left it near the front door. When Vicky saw my bag, she asked, "You're not leaving yet, Nana, are you?"

"No, baby," I said, "but I will be leaving as soon as breakfast is done and I have told you the next adventure."

Going Home for Christmas
Chapter 5

Ava was an accomplished pianist at thirteen, not to cite her artistic talents, which were in such demand for all the Christmas concerts and posters. Secluded in the music cottage I would crack my knuckles; pound the keys, pretending I was performing at a great concert; and then revert to my boring scales. On one of these occasions while in the throes of a so-called Mozart concerto, Ava burst into the cottage, proclaiming how awful it sounded to her and probably everyone in the immediate area. I jumped up from my piano stool and looked out the window to see if anyone else might have heard. Instead, she started playing a beautiful melody and told me to sing along with the lyrics she handed me. "Me, sing? I don't think so," I told her. When I refused, she grabbed me by my skirt and yanked me to the piano, making a menacing fist. I immediately cleared my throat, ready to sing.

    I asked her to sing the lyrics first so I could hear how I was supposed to sound. Her voice changed to a very sad but angelic tone as she obliged. I found that I was holding my breath through the whole song, and when she was finished I let out a big sigh. She changed back to her normal, bullying self and ordered, "You sing it just like that." I told her it was so beautiful, but I could never sing it just like her. She looked up at me sternly when I noticed she had tears forming in her eyes. "OK, I'll try" I said.

    It started with the chorus, and then the verse followed by the chorus again. I sang it a couple of times, when she finally slammed her hands on the keys. She turned her body to face me, grabbed me by the arms, and shook me. "I composed this song because it is very special to me. Imagine what it would be like if someone you loved very much should die, leaving you all alone in the world. Now sing it again," she yelled. She was thinking of our dad, but I thought of my Jesus.

The song was about my papa after all, and it did not have to be about an earthly father. I thought how Jesus had already died for me, yet He was still alive. I thought, *After all, I do talk to Him a lot, especially during Communion*. I thought how terrible it would be if I could never see Him again or be able to ever talk to Him again. I was now ready to sing her song.

My Papa

My Papa, my Papa, come back to me.
My Papa, my Papa, come back to me.
My Papa, my Papa, come back to me.
Oh, I need you, I need you I do.
When you went away, I was just a babe,
Crying in Mama's arms all day.
You took me and you held me as I was told,
Oh, your arms were an ocean of gold.
Chorus
Now I am big and I understand,
What it is to go on without your hand.
You guided my footsteps when I took them first,
But now you are not there to trust.
Chorus
Praise be to God and His will be done,
He must have sent you, only that I'd be born.
Now I am here, but you are gone.
Oh, when will I meet you in the eternal dawn.
Chorus

I was now so deep into the song with tears rolling down my face that even started Ava sniffling as she whispered, "Good." She was finally satisfied and got up from the piano, telling me to go with her to see Mother Virginia. We ran through the passageway under the south balcony and made a sharp turn right. Ava grabbed me by the wrist and dragged me up the stairs to the end of the assembly balcony to the last classroom.

I was so out of breath when we got there that I could not have sung to save my life. This was to be Ava's contribution to our Christmas show, and she couldn't wait to spring it on our music teacher. The last classroom near the nuns' refectory also had a piano, where Mother Virginia practiced with the choirgirls. She turned to see us both enter the room and pointed at me, asking, "Why aren't you using this hour to practice your scales?" when Ava jumped in front of me with a joyous, "Surprise!" She began explaining why I was there and that she wanted her to hear something. Mother Virginia moved away from the piano bench and pointed to it. Ava slipped onto it, pulling me next to her, nodding to start. I took the lyrics page out of my pocket and smoothed out the creases, trying to get back into the same frame of mind. *My Jesus,* I thought, *this is for You.* Ava played, and I sang.

Mother Virginia had a big smile on her face and stood with one hand on each of our shoulders. She turned my face upward to her and told me that I had a beautiful voice, just what she needed in her choir. I was to stay there for practice until the rest of the girls arrived and practice my scales. She then turned to Ava and patted her on the head. "I'm very proud of your accomplishment; we will definitely include it in our Christmas concert. I want you both to practice this every day until Tess knows all the words, but I want it to be a duet. I want you to sing it in harmony." Ava told her she couldn't play and sing, but Mother Virginia insisted.

I finally had an opportunity to join the choir and found very little time to practice the piano between rehearsals. The concert was approaching, and the show must go on. I told Anna how nervous I was to get up in front of the whole school to sing, and I wished I could get a sore throat or something. Anna always made me laugh or feel good, especially when she made me realize that I was like the little drummer boy. She explained that I should sing the song to Jesus as though I were right there in the manger at His birth. I was to imagine Mary and Joseph kneeling near the baby while I sang my present to him. She helped me memorize the words, which made it easier to sing from my heart.

I went back to my piano practice at the cottage, and we rehearsed a couple of times a week. It felt strange to regain my solitude in the music cottage, but I would frequently find myself still singing the song in my head. I would stand in front of some barrels that were stored in the back and front room, pretending they were the audience to whom I would curtsey as I imagined their applause. I did this every day until one day my curiosity about the barrels got the better of me. I lifted the heavy wooden lid, and lo and behold it was full of dried, pickled mango strips. My jaws ached with saliva dripping into my throat through my hour of scales.

"Just one piece would do it," I thought. I jumped up from the piano stool and dashed to a barrel and looked over my shoulder, expecting to be spied upon, and I pinched a piece. I rushed back to the piano and cradled the mango piece in my hand, wondering if they would miss one piece out of all those barrels. I brought it to my lips and tasted the salt, taking a tiny bite off the end. I drooled with pleasure and just popped the whole shriveled up piece into my mouth. It tasted so wonderful that I just couldn't resist chewing it. To my dismay it was gone too soon; I had to have more. I looked out the window to see if anyone was close enough to watch me and then ran to another barrel, taking another piece. This time I popped it into my mouth without hesitation. I decided that this was it. No more.

Something inside of me was telling me I was committing a terrible sin of stealing, and I would have to go to confession; but, I also thought that the nuns had so much of it, why couldn't they share? It felt like I had a devil on my left shoulder and an angel on my right. I picked up my books and ran to find Anna, who was always busy at her sewing machine. I was glad the angel won, yet I felt so bad inside. I sat on the floor fidgeting until she looked over her glasses at me.

"What's bothering you?" she asked with a smile.
"Nothing," I replied, not looking at her.
"What did you do?"
"Nothing," I replied again with tears welling up. She got up from the sewing machine and came to sit on the floor with me. She put her arm around my shoulders and assured me that it would be all right. I leaned into her while I cried, telling her between sobs that I had stolen two pieces of mango from the music cottage barrels. I was afraid that Jesus would be so mad at me. Father Anthony would not be at church to hear confession until Friday, and today was only Tuesday. My stomach hurt so badly, and I wished I had never

touched those barrels. Anna hugged me and stood up, pulling me to my feet. She told me that I had already confessed my sin by telling her and that she knew Jesus would have forgiven me already. I asked, "How do you know this, Anna?" She went on to explain that Jesus knew that I was sorry because I had all the symptoms, such as a stomachache and the remorse and willpower never to do it again. I still felt it was not official enough unless a priest would give me penance and bless me with forgiveness in Jesus's name. I felt better when I left Anna, but the urgency of confession on Friday still ate at my heart.

It was Wednesday, and I did not take Communion. I learned that I could not receive Communion if I had sinned. I watched everyone else receiving it, and I longed to have Him visit me again, but I dared not. I felt so ashamed to be in church just in case He could see me through the mouths of the two girls on either side of me. Mother Doris had always said that when we sinned, our hearts became black with the devil, and Jesus could not enter there when it was dirty. I felt like tearing out my heart to clean it, but knew I had to wait until Friday.

Thursday I didn't practice my piano at the cottage. Instead I insisted that Ava and I practice her song for the concert at the choir piano. It was Friday at last, and I was first in line at the confessionals. Father Anthony heard my confession. "Father, I sinned on Tuesday and have had the worst week because I could not get to you until today." I told him I had stolen two pieces of pickled mango and promised I'd never steal anything ever again. It felt so good to get it off my chest, and I actually felt the darkness lift from my soul. Father Anthony explained that since he represented Jesus and would take my sins to Him, I should know I was already forgiven. He told me to say three Our Father's and three Hail Mary's for penance and blessed me with forgiveness. Whew! What a relief. My heart felt light, and my soul was white once more. I could visit Jesus again and wondered if He would remember what I had done.

I was skipping along to the dormitory when I ran into Mina, who was struggling with her shoelaces. I grabbed her from behind and scared her into squealing. I bent down and tied her laces and told her that she was a big girl now and needed to know how not to get her thumb caught into the bow. We sat on the wash wall and practiced tying her laces until she got it right. She laughed so heartily and wanted to run and tell everyone that she could tie her laces all by herself. Mina had turned five in November and could not wait to go into the first standard (or grade) after the holidays.

It was almost the last week before school shut down for the Christmas holidays. Everyone seemed so busy getting the two classrooms next to the dormitory ready. The wall that separated the classes was just a partition and easily taken down. The rooms became one gigantic hall with a platform for a stage. Mother Virginia's piano was rolled all along the nuns' living quarters then through Anna's room to the long hallway and then into the stage room. Ava was busying herself drawing posters and back stage scenes for other skits, and it seemed that there was nothing for me to do but stand and watch.

At playtime that night Mother Doris called out the names of girls that were going home for the Christmas holidays, and I was so happy when Ava and I were also mentioned. I didn't know whether to jump for joy or be scared or sad. My emotions just fell into whatever Ava was feeling, and she was rejoicing. We could only pack a small bag of essentials and report to Mother Superior at the end of the week for her instructions on how and when the trip would take place. I started daydreaming how wonderful it would be to see the ocean, swing in the garden, and build sand castles on the beach. I was getting excited to the point of uncontrolled jitters and could not wait to tell Anna about it.

Instead, when I turned I looked into Mina's sad face I saw big, swollen tears just about to drop. I hugged her and took her aside, telling her that I would bring her back a present and lots of candy and bubble gum. Our supply had long since depleted, and we were once again saving wads of used gum under our beds. She didn't smile but just burst out crying. I realized then that I had never taken the time to find out anything about Mina's life and had just used her as a sidekick friend. It was almost like what Ava did with me, but I really loved Mina and could not be cruel to her. I had no idea how lonely she must have been at that moment, knowing that almost all the boarders were going away in just a week. I was about to ask her about her parents when the bell rang, and it was time for the rosary and bed. I hugged her again and told her to make sure and go to the bathroom before bed and follow the usual nightly run when I would wake her. She sadly nodded and left for her dormitory, while I went to mine.

Mother Doris was already kneeling with all the girls, so I ran to my bed and knelt down too. I prayed the words with my mouth while my heart was still wondering about Mina. Maybe Anna knew something about her family, because Anna knew everything. I attached my mosquito net, changed into my pajamas, and slipped under my sheet, trying to sleep.

My mind would not stop racing with thoughts of Mummy and home, leaving Anna and Mina, and just anticipating the train journey home. I did finally fall asleep but was awakened by someone's hand inside my net shaking me.

    I opened my eyes and looked out of the opening to see Mina standing there. It was so dark that I could hardly see all of her. I got out of bed to ask her what was wrong when she cupped her hands around my ear and whispered. Amongst her sobs, I heard her say she had forgotten to go to the bathroom after the rosary and had wet her bed. My stomach started hurting, as usual; Mina had been dry for so many months that I felt responsible for not having taken her there myself before lights out. I put my hands on her shoulders and quietly guided her back to her dormitory. I stripped her bed sheets and opened the cupboard that had clean ones. I quickly changed sheets and took her nightgown off. I opened her locker and gave her a clean change of clothes, while I decided to go to the bathroom and dump the wet ones into the Dhobi box. I tucked her in and saw her beautiful smile again.

    Mother Doris stepped out of the bathroom stall, catching me red handed at the Dhobi box. I was so surprised to see her that I dropped all the wet clothes into the box, letting the lid slam with a loud noise. I looked up at her now-approaching white gown, and her hand rose above her head. She did not say a word while her face changed into a terrifying, twisted look, the same look I had seen on Mummy when she burned my hands. Her cane came crashing down across my face and chest. I felt a welt the length of my face swell, while my heart leapt out of my mouth in a silent scream. I knelt down at her feet and covered my head and face with my arms, telling her I was sorry for disobeying her rules, but she continued whipping my arms with the cane.

    She still did not speak a word but grabbed me by my neck and forced me into the Dhobi box. She lifted the lid and, with the cane, motioned me to climb into it. I covered my head with my arms to shield it from the blows while I rolled over into the box. I was so glad when she brought the lid down over me, which stopped the cane stings. I buried my face into the wet sheets, when to my horror I heard her bolt the box shut. She spoke with such an evil, angry voice, "Now stay there till I come for you in the morning. If anyone comes in to use the bathroom, you are not to speak a word, or you will stay there all day too!"

    The heavy mesh covering the lid to allow air into the box was now tightly shut. I waited in silence listening to her footsteps disappear in the distance. I pushed on the lid with my back arched, hoping the latch would move and allow me to stand up. The suffocating smells from the dirty clothes grew pungent and attached to my nightgown, my skin, and hair. Not knowing how many hours had gone by, I felt my face and arms swell while my skin burned feverishly. I picked up the wet sheet and dabbed it to my face, to cool it down. I found I could not stretch my legs and started to panic. I kicked as many of the clothes to one side of the box, but they only ended over my head, making me feel as if I were being buried alive. I wanted to scream but could not in fear that I might attract the cane once more. I fought with the dirty clothes all night and finally passed out through exhaustion.

    When morning finally came, I heard Mother Doris undo the bolt and the lid flew open, with me jumping out like a Jack-in-the-box. I stood there up to my waist in smelly clothes while she lectured me about my rule-breaking. I had learned never to fight back since it only brought more pain. I got out at her request and knelt before her, saying, "Thank you, Mother, for the punishment. I deserved it." She walked away while I ran to my bed.

I picked up my basin and went to the wash wall, trying to wash my whole body in five inches of water. While I dressed for mass I got curious looks from the other girls. When Ava passed me on her way to line up, she put her hand to her mouth and looked at me with the saddest eyes. The concert was next week. *How ugly I would look with this mark on my face,* I thought. It didn't matter that my arms were marked, but my face? I could never sing in public looking like that. Maybe Ava could sing, and I would stand behind the curtain to harmonize.

Mother Doris was outside ringing the bell for the line up. I grabbed my veil and prayer book and ran to get in line. In church that morning I sat next to a very shocked Anna, who didn't pinch me because she was afraid she might hurt me. She had tears in her eyes as she leaned into me, and I leaned back to acknowledge her. I knelt down very carefully to avoid the painful parts while I held my most precious cargo in my mouth. I found myself climbing up over my teeth, trying to reach my beautiful Jesus. He reached out His hand and lifted me into His arms, where I lay my tired head on His shoulder. It felt so good to just lie there while He rubbed my head and back in a soothing way. I lifted my head and looked Him right in the eyes, and then He spoke: "It will pass, Tess." I hugged His neck and told Him not to let me go back; I wanted to go with Him. I felt so safe and warm in His arms that I held on so tight.

"Please, Jesus. Don't put me down," I cried.

Jesus sat down with me in His lap and said, "Remember, Tess. I am always with you, and I love you very much."

My eyes opened to Anna, helping me off my knees and smiling at me. I looked around and saw Mother Doris in the back of the chapel talking to Mother Superior. I was just glad she was far away, and I could whisper to Anna. I kept my eyes on Mother Doris while I told Anna briefly what had happened that night and how I wished I had died just then to go with Jesus. Anna patted my hand and rubbed my kneecap, the only place on my body that didn't hurt, telling me that everything would be all right. She told me to come see her after breakfast, and she would put something on my face to take away the red marks and the pain. I felt better knowing she was there, and I told her so. I turned back to the front when I saw Mother Doris returning to her seat and knew the conversation with Anna had to end.

"Anna, why does Mother Doris hurt kids so much? Does she hate us? Is she not supposed to be holy? Do you think Jesus will forgive her for hurting me?" I went on asking.

Anna couldn't answer any of those questions until I sat down and let her apply the salve all over my welts. She finally finished and said, "Mother Doris is answerable only to God for the way she treats the children. We need to pray for her to change, but even if she doesn't, then God will take care of it. She was here at the convent when I arrived, and I think she was here even as a child, you know, as an orphan. The nuns took care of her, and when she finished school she became a nun. Mother Superior put her in charge of the kids because she had spent all her childhood as a boarder and had the experience.

"Sometimes people become nuns for the wrong reasons, and I cannot tell you if it is because they are holy or not. Enough questions for now. Take my towel and wash up. You really smell sour."

"You know so much, Anna," I said as I walked to her sink. "Do you know anything about Mina?" She busied herself by putting the medicine away and said her name aloud—"Mina"—trying to remember. "Mina is the little outcast."

"What's that?" I asked.

"Well, her mother was an Indian, and her father was an English soldier. He loved Mina's mother but had to leave with his regiment when they went back to England but couldn't take her with him. She told the nuns that he promised to come back for her and the baby someday. Her family would have stoned Mina's mother to death if they found out that she was going to have a baby without getting married, so she came to the nuns for help. When Mina was born her mother went back to her family. In a way, Mina is just like Mother Doris, an orphan, and most probably, if not adopted, she will become a nun also."

I shivered at the thought of poor Mina ever becoming as horrid as Mother Doris. I said, "Anna, if Mother Doris was treated very badly when she was a border, does it mean that all kids when they grow up treat others badly too?"

"I don't know, Tess. I think if you stay angry without finding a way to forgive them for hurting you, you might end up staying angry all your life and, in turn, hurt someone else because you believe that to be the only way. If Jesus can forgive us our sins, don't you think we should forgive those who hurt us too?"

I nodded and asked, "Anna, can I stay angry for a little while longer before forgiving Mother Doris?" She smiled and said it was all right.

I looked into her mirror, saw the stripe across my face, and raised my arms to discover more stripes. Anna reminded me that Jesus was beaten a hundred times more but had no one to put medicine on His wounds. I hugged my Anna and told her she was my special angel, just like in the picture she gave me for my birthday, and would love her forever. I guess my tears were flowing, and she said she loved me too.

"Now wipe away those zebra tears, Tess, and come see me after school." I realized that I did look like a zebra and wondered how I would explain it to my friends, the day scholars.

***

"Oh, Mom," cried Becky, "I'm so sorry for the horrible time you had as a child. Now I understand why you never left us with anyone and kept us close to you. Thanks, Mom!" With that I got a loving hug. The next thing I knew the kids were all over me with hugs and kisses, thanking me for being their Nanny Nana while they grew up too. "I just had to change things for us," I said, "and to make sure that my children and grandchildren never had to experience this type of abuse but just the opposite, with lots and lots of love. I'm so happy that you all turned out OK."

"Nana, when do you go home for Christmas in this story?" asked Vicky.

"Soon," I answered.

"Can we go on then?"

***

It was concert day at last. Day scholars and their families were arriving, while the nuns ushered them to their seats. Ava was playing all the songs she had learned to entertain the crowds, and frantic preparations were going on behind the scenes. Mother Virginia almost lost her headgear when she ducked under a low curtain rope, and with one hand on her head she tried to zip up the wings on a fallen angel. The orderly confusion made quite a humorous show itself.

I hid in a corner of the backstage with a good view of all the performances. Ava and I were to end the show with our song. Mother Virginia finally approached me with a big smile and lifted my chin. She turned my head from one side to another, and I realized she was looking at the now-fading stripe across my face. She waved down a nun who was helping with the costumes and make-up and spoke in Latin to her. I guess she didn't want me to understand what she was saying. I was given a complete facial that made me look beautiful, while the long sleeved white gown covered my striped arms.

First, the choir sang praises in a medley of hymns, which was followed by the Nativity play. Mina was one of the angels and looked so adorable flitting about. Ava played the part of Mary, wearing a nun's habit for her costume that made her look so beautiful. Ava was in quite a few of the plays and had her own personal nun to help her change into the various costumes. I sat on a tall stool through the whole show until it was nearly my turn. My stomach hurt a little, so

I made my way to the side door and started breathing in the fresh air in big gulps. I was suddenly feeling too confined in one place and had to feel the freedom of the open air. I stepped out into the now empty hallway and peeked into the concert hall. I recognized some of my day scholar friends when they pointed to me to tell their parents who I was, I guess about how they had created the spice monster.

 I backed away in shyness and started toward the stage entrance when I felt a hand on my shoulder. I turned around, and it was Anna. She had seen me from the audience and wanted to come and wish me all the best. She hugged me and told me where she was standing and to look all the way in the back against the wall. She reminded me how wonderful I sounded and that Jesus was going to love His present. I hugged her back and snuck back behind stage. I went to the curtain and peeked and saw her walking past the other people without seats to lean up against the wall.

 Ava pulled on my arm to join her center stage. Our gowns straightened and faces touched up, we heard Mother Virginia introduce the last act and its author. A duet composed by Ava, age thirteen, accompanied by her sister Tess: "My Papa." The curtain pulled away slowly to expose the ocean of faces. I took a deep breath and saw Anna wave to me. I kept my eyes on her, while in my mind I pictured myself dressed like the little drummer boy, trump-pum-pum.

 It was over as fast as it had begun. Parents in the audience with their children swarmed the stage to shake our hands. Some embraced us, some pinched my cheeks, and they were all over us. I broke out into a cold sweat. It felt just like being in the Dhobi box! They all smelled from their own brands of perfumes, which nauseated me. I fell to my knees and crawled for the doors from right between their legs. Ava enjoyed the limelight, while I thought, "She can have it!"

The next morning Mother Superior called all the older girls into her office and handed them the tickets and schedule of trains. I had nothing to worry about: just be there when the bus leaves for the station.

Anna found me sitting with Mina on the wash-up wall. She came and sat down next to us and handed Mina a cute cloth doll she had made. Mina did not take it but let it drop to the floor. I bent down to pick it up at the same time Anna did, almost bumping heads. We laughed and hugged while Anna took the doll and patted its head, made the doll jump on her lap and somersault by throwing it up into the air. I never saw Anna act so silly, but I also knew Anna never did anything unless it was for a good reason. I looked at Mina, who had developed a smile while watching the performance. Anna never said a word through all of this.

I glanced at her as she captivated Mina's full attention, then giving me a nudge to disappear. Anna was so smart. I made an excuse that I heard Ava call me and told them I would be back. I ran to my dormitory and peeked through the crack in the door. It looked like Anna was talking now, and Mina was responding with nodding yes and no. I was happy for Mina and felt peace of mind. I left them alone to go finish my packing.

We had to roll up our mattress and empty out our lockers, because when we got back we might not have the same bed assigned to us. I had to put my basin on the bedsprings facedown so that the number could be seen. I remembered all the bubble gum stuck on the frame of the bed and started pulling them off; no telling what would have happened if Mother Doris saw that. I was now all packed and ready for our trip. In just a couple of hours we would be boarding the school bus to leave the convent walls to freedom!

I went looking for Anna and Mina, who were not where I had left them. I knocked on Anna's door, and Mina opened it. She was her old, happy self and had taken over for me. I looked at Anna, who was at the sewing machine, while Mina kept babbling about Anna making her new doll another dress. I patted her on the head and made a beeline for Anna. She stood up and held up the tiny blue school uniform for the doll. Mina squealed and grabbed it out of her hand. She sat on the floor and immediately started removing the plain white dress in exchange for the uniform.

I put my arm around Anna and squeezed her tight. I had to whisper that it was time for me to leave and that I would miss her so much. She just hugged me back and whispered, "I won't miss you." She looked at my puzzled face and went on to say, "You can't miss me if you remember me; it will be like I was with you," she smiled. I hugged her again, bent down to kiss Mina on the top of her head, and slipped away. Once outside Anna's room, I leaned back on the closed door. I took a last look at both ends of the hallway and walked under the bell. I jumped and touched it, making it ring ever so lightly. I smiled and felt that I had survived a year, wondering what was in store for me once we left the confines of the convent, even if for just a few weeks.

How can I describe this giant of a man named Pasco? He was the convent's bus driver and handyman, who took care of the school's transportation needs. We never saw the bus parked on the property and assumed he had it in a garage off site. I sat at the very back of the bus and looked out the window thinking I might get a last glimpse of Anna or Mina. I saw the few girls left behind waving to us, feeling so sorry for them. I wondered what Christmas would be like for them, alone, without a family.

Some parents, a week before, had collected the rich girls who didn't care if our Christmas concert was missed. I could not imagine the type of holiday rich girls had, but then Anna always said, "If you don't know, you won't miss it." I understood now what she meant.

I had never ridden on a school bus or experienced Pasco's driving before that day. He thought he would have some fun with the girls and started weaving the bus to make us fall out of our seats. I was so scared that I clung to the side handle and braced my back against the seat by pushing my legs up against the seat in front. The girls were in a great holiday mood, singing and laughing at Pasco's antics, increasing the celebration. I smiled and sang along while still seated, ready for a crash. "Please get us to the station in one piece, Lord," I prayed, and then burst into a chorus of Jingle Bells. The school was out of sight and hopefully out of mind.

We had arrived at the station so soon, nothing like the first ride in the dumni that seemed to have taken an eternity. I stayed on the bus with the other kids my age while the older ones, led by Pasco, handled all the compartment arrangements. The station manager gave Pasco three large signs that said Reserved to hang out of our compartment window. This would secure our compartments from intruders through all the stops with the aid of each station manager right on through to Bombay. Pasco came on board to make sure everyone was accounted for and to check that each compartment had a designated leader. There was to be no switching of compartments, as those were the rules set by Mother Superior. Still more rules, but these were sensible enough even for me.

    The whistle blew, and the train jerked forward. We were finally on our way, with the girls claiming their territory for the duration of the long ride. Our compartment had about sixteen to twenty girls, most of them much older than I. I leaned out the window remembering the last experience of the smell of coal, the wind in my hair, and humming to the sound of the wheels clanking along. I finally turned around to see everyone in their seats either talking to one another, reading, or some in a group singing. I felt so exhilarated with the thoughts of a new adventure ahead that I didn't care I had no window seat.

    I looked up at the baggage rack, noticing how wide and roomy it was. I checked the chains holding it up on each end, and they felt quite secure. I got a wonderful feeling of wanting to climb up high pretending it was a tall tree. I asked Ava and some of the big girls there to give me a push up, and now I had secured my territory. Using my little bag as a pillow, I lay in the baggage rack with my eyes closed listening to the girls talk about what they were going to do when they got home. I started imagining how wonderful it would be to see our beloved beach home and watch those beautiful sunsets. Some started planning to get off at one of the stations to buy romance novels. They were working out a plan by checking their watches for the next few stations and watched each platform where there might be a paper or bookstand. They discovered that every station so far had a kiosk in about the same place, and if the next stop had one they would jump out, money ready, and dash back, timing it just right.

The train started slowing down, my heart started beating faster, and my stomach began to churn. I opened my eyes and swung down from the baggage rack, just barely reaching the seat and then the floor. The deal was, if there were many people in front of the stand, we were to come right back for another attempt at the next station. If there was to be a choice of books, just grab a variety and move fast. Ava decided that she would stay leaning out of the train window to yell with encouragement rather than run with them. My stomach stopped hurting immediately when I heard that, but my heart kept beating so fast I thought I would have to put my hands to my mouth in case it decided to leave my body.

"Ready?" The train stopped. "Get set!" we all shouted. Bookstand sighted—"Go!" The two girls chosen dashed out the door to the stand while Ava and the rest of us started shouting, "Hurry, hurry, hurry, hurry." My heart jumped with every "hurry" while I watched through the other sea of heads and bodies sticking out the windows all shouting in unison, "Hurry, hurry, hurry, hurry." We felt the jolt of the train as we yelled, faster now, "Hurry," and finally the door opened and shut with a slam! Whew! They all let out a tremendous scream of relief and pleasure, while there was a mad scramble for long-awaited forbidden romance novels.

I found myself taking deep breaths to bring my heart into rhythm with the wheels once more. The compartment was silent again, even though some of the girls, in excited but hushed tones, nudged each other about what they had discovered in their books. I leaned out the window, closed my eyes, and began humming "My Papa" to the accompaniment of the wheels. *How peaceful it was*, I thought, and my mind wandered to Anna and Mina, wondering how they were doing. How I wished they could have been there to enjoy this moment with me. According to Anna, she was, because I was thinking of her.

Lunch consisted of an egg sandwich and a banana. I took my lunch with me to the bathroom, where I saw a sink with running water and a beautiful commode. Wow! I put the seat cover down and sat on it to eat my sandwich, saving my banana for later. I put the banana down on the toilet seat and ran cold water over my hands, cupping them together and quickly drinking before it fell through my fingers. It felt so good when I washed my face and arms, and I did not care that I had no towel. I finally left the bathroom and went back to the window, tossing my banana up into the rack for later. The wind blew my face and arms dry while I sat on the edge of my seat watching the countryside go by.

After a while I decided to people watch. I saw many Indian people going about their business, unaware of my eyes intruding into their private lives. Not much I could call exciting, but it was more of a pitiful sight. There were families with huge bundles tied up over their heads, a father with a small bundle on his head with his wife who had their little baby girl on her hip, and towing their son who could scarcely walk. I watched them look for a compartment that was not too full, all while hampered with their bundles and children and trying to board the train. I stretched my neck a great deal out of the window to tag along with my eyes. They finally did get on, just as the train jerked forward.

Under protest of putting down their books, a couple

of the girls gave me a hoist up to the baggage rack and threatened me to stay put for the evening. I smiled and rolled over onto my side facing the train wall, when I realized I had just squashed my banana! I jumped up and hit my head into the ceiling and fell back onto the banana, yelling, "Ouch, ouch, ouch!" I finally settled down and picked banana off my clothes and ate whatever I could rescue. Then I leaned over the edge and flung the banana skin out the window to land someplace, to probably be kicked around by some Indian kids with no inkling of the story behind that banana or where it came from. I decided to take a short nap until dinner, hoping it would be something more appetizing than an egg sandwich.

    I awoke to a sudden jerk, as the train came to an unscheduled screeching stop. I leaned over to look out the window, but it was pitch black. I noticed the other girls also had the same idea to discover what had happened. Under threats of losing the opportunity of ever getting back to the rack, I once again slipped down from my sanctuary to join the girls in this curiosity. A train engineer was waving a lantern, yelling inaudibly to the other end of the train. In synchronization, we all turned to look at the other lantern waving back but heard nothing. We returned to just waiting it out when one of the leaders from the other compartment hollered out her window to us. We now had window communication passed on from the front of the train, until it finally reached us.

    The story we got was that there was a sacred cow sitting on the tracks, as people were frantically trying to coax it to move. I learned that some Indian religions worshiped cows, and the train was to remain there until their god decided to leave. We kept getting news flashes passed down to us for the next couple of hours, when finally we heard shouts of cheering coming in waves through the night air. The train jerked forward again, and we all stared out into the darkness to see this amazing cow that was able to hold up a train for his holiness.

I waited patiently for my turn at a sandwich and watched someone start eating theirs, noticing the familiar egg white. Oh well, something was better than nothing, I thought. My sandwich could have been eaten in just two bites, but I was happy to see a good-looking banana that I consumed right after the main course. I made my bathroom rounds and washed up again. I passed some girls engrossed in their third or fourth novel by now, while others slept, stretched out on the bench seats.

Ava and another girl were trying different hairstyles, when suddenly I was grabbed into their midst. "Tess, don't you want to look pretty for Mummy?" I nodded and let them give me a haircut. The other girl directed her on how much to cut on each side so it would look even. Finally, I stood up and watched my beautiful long hair fall to the floor. She looked at me, saying, "Great cut, Tess. Go look in the bathroom mirror." I did what she asked, believing I looked pretty only because my big sister said so. I quietly went to the window near my baggage rack, put one foot on the seat between a sleeping girl and the window, put the other foot on the window sill, and then pulled myself up on the chain holding the rack. I swung the other foot up to the rack and rolled over onto it. My neck was itching now, and I kept dusting off the invisible hair responsible for the inconvenience and hoped Mummy would like my new hairstyle.

Ava was shaking me awake, saying, "Bombay is next.

Get up." I awoke and saw daylight. The girls were grooming themselves and packing up what they had used on the trip. I quickly gathered the contents that had fallen out of my little bag and shoved them back in. I then grabbed the chain, stepped on the window, letting myself down onto the seat, and made a dash for the bathroom. I pounded on the door and heard someone yell, "In a minute." I jumped up and down, paced back and forth until the door finally opened, and I rushed in and shut the door. I looked into the little broken mirror over the sink and noticed I had coal dust smeared on my face, and my hair was a mess. I washed and brushed my teeth, but having no comb or long hair I just wet and fingered my hair into place. I got out of there as fast as I could because I felt the train slowing down.

There was no room at any of the windows, as the girls were anxiously looking through the crowds trying to pick out their parents who had come for them. I looked up and saw the sign approaching the station. It read "Bombay."

I heard Ava shout, "Mummy, Mummy! Over here!" I grabbed her by the skirt to make sure I wasn't separated or left behind. I jumped off the train, keeping my eyes on Ava until she led us to Mummy. There she was, standing in the shade of an umbrella, waving to us. Ava jumped into her arms and hugged her while I waited my turn. She looked down at me and then touched my hair, while I gave her the biggest smile I had, feeling so pretty because Ava said I was.

She bent and hugged me, saying, "What have you done to your pretty hair?" My smile faded immediately as Mummy said, "Stay close together, now. We have a taxi waiting."

I picked up my bag and followed them, thinking how

Ava had once again deceived me. Why did she hate me so much?

I jumped out of the taxi as soon as it stopped, trying to beat Ava to the entrance, but she always won. We waited in the doorway for Mummy to come in and our *aya* (servant) was helping her bring in our bags. Someone above us shyly said, "Hello down there," and we looked up to find four girls between the ages of five to fourteen smiling down at us. I waved back and said hello, and so did Ava. We looked at each other for a few minutes, not knowing who they were, when Mummy walked up to us and waved to them too. She invited them to come meet her daughters. They were our neighbors on the second floor who had moved in since our send-off to boarding school. Yasmin was fourteen, Diana was twelve, Roda was ten, and Veera was five. Ava and Yasmin were the closest in age, while Roda and I were almost the same. Diana and Veera were the odd ones out, but I adored Veera, who reminded me so much of Mina.

Everyone was in the big hall sitting on the floor learning about each other, and I suddenly remembered the beach and asked if they wanted to go swimming with us. Mummy called their mother, who said it would be no problem, but their *aya* would join us to keep an eye on Veera. We all squealed with joy, and in no time at all there were six laughing and screaming kids in the house. I really felt our holiday had finally begun.

I stood at the same window that I had dreamed about in school and saw the shiny sparkles dance on the water in the distance. I quickly pulled off my dress and just left on my knickers and petticoat, kicking off my shoes and socks. The cold mosaic floor felt so wonderfully familiar that I rubbed my bare feet over it in a friendly hello. I turned to leave the room and dash down to the promenade when I stopped dead in my tracks. I was in the front foyer, where the kids had all gathered to wait for their *aya*. There was something wrong! I ran into the main hall, and there, too, Daddy was gone!

I screamed for Mummy, pointing to the walls. "Where are all Daddy's paintings?" Ava looked around and suddenly noticed they were gone too. All the beautiful murals that represented a living inheritance were whitewashed over. Mummy told us to go swimming with our new friends, and later she would talk about it. I couldn't believe how empty it made me feel, nor could I imagine the angry thoughts that were beginning to erupt within my sister.

Roda and I raced to the promenade, leaving the rest behind. Aya had Veera by her hand, protecting her every step; she was being treated like a little princess, but she struggled to get free of the hand that held her captive. We sat on the promenade wall, then climbed over the edge and jumped. What an exhilarating experience being airborne and landing on the soft sand below. I sat in the cool sand and dug my feet into it, waiting for the others to catch up. I pulled my head back and closed my eyes, taking in a deep breath of the sea breeze.

"Bhel!" I cried out. "I smell bhel!" I yelled again. Ava stood above me like a tall tower and pulled me up by the neck of my petticoat, saying, "Get in the water. I'll race you." She ran behind me as we joined the others. There were high and glorious waves, perfect for jumping through. Veera sat at the edge of the water with her *aya* and began building sand castles. In and out we bobbed through the waves, catching our breath just in time before the next one to hit. How I had missed it all. Roda made her way next to me so we could hold hands to help each other in case a big one overcame us.

The high-spirited fun went on for so long that I didn't notice Aya waving at us to come in. I bobbed up from under a big wave and noticed the girls had started moving back to shore. My attention was grabbed by a tremendous wave that knocked me under, leaving me to struggle to the surface. I felt I had been pulled deeper, and a weight was on my back that almost pinned my face into the sandy bottom. I had now run out of breath and struggled frantically to get back to the surface for air. I felt as though someone was standing on my back pushing me down to hold me there. I was again in the Dhobi box with no hope of escape!

Suddenly a hand grabbed me by the leg and started pulling me up. I felt the pressure from my back lift, and I was free to kick my legs into the sand to boost me out of the waves and into the precious air. I took a big gulp, only to be knocked over by another wave. I saw Ava was just a little way in front of me making her way out to the beach. I used the next wave to propel me toward shore, which brought me crashing on top of her. She went down like a rock, and I couldn't see her anywhere. I was now so terrified I developed a cramp in my stomach. I had to find her! I felt her limp body being tossed around with the current under my feet, so I grabbed her by her waist with my feet and began to pull her up. Once I could reach her with my hands, I pulled her face out of the water. She started coughing while I held onto her till she regained her breath. She gave me such a scared look, as though she had either met God or the devil! She pulled away from me and dashed for shore, leaving me to struggle to safety.

Ava was lying on her tummy still coughing up the sea, and the *aya* was patting her on the back to aid the process. I pulled myself onto the shore and lay down to regain my strength. Roda came and sat next to me. "What happened to you, Tess. Did you get hit by a big one? I was so worried when I couldn't see you anywhere in the water. Yasmin swam out to find you, but Ava said that she would look for you."

I managed to smile and said, "She found me, alright."

"Good," said Roda, and she started telling me that Aya was taking us all to eat bhel as soon as we had recovered.

After such a vigorous swim and our stomachs empty of rations since dinner on the train, I could have eaten every scrap that was on the bhel wagon. The man handed me the bhel neatly laid out on a banana leaf, when the smell just overcame my anxiously waiting stomach. I dug right in and ate gulps of it at a time. I looked at the others all eating it so daintily while I pigged out. They were all laughing at me. Even Ava smiled. Aya remarked that she had never seen anyone finish a bhel so fast, but I didn't care. It was so good.

After that wonderful treat, Aya told the man to open up six coconuts, and we all lay on the beach drinking the cool milk and munching on the soft, deliciously sweet coconut meat. I was so full now that I gave Ava the rest of my coconut, which she seemed to be enjoying almost as much as I did the bhel.

After such an exhausting afternoon, Mummy suggested we take a nap. We discovered that it was an everyday occurrence that Mummy took an afternoon rest. We didn't complain; instead we looked forward to just sleeping in a comfortable bed with our belly full. Our newfound friends went home and promised they would return to play with us later that evening. There was much to look forward to, but sleep took precedence.

    The smell of home cooking woke me from a deep sleep. Yummy onions, garlic, turmeric, fresh cooked rice, and *dahl* (red lentils). I sat upright in bed, only to discover that it was already dark outside. I had slept through the whole evening and failed to notice my first sunset. The steeples of Mount Mary's Church glowed in the now darkening sky, leaving a streak of white light over the water, which had calmed in comparison to that afternoon. I heard the soft whoosh of the calm waves now breaking against the shoreline. The lights along the two sides of land bore a resemblance to a diamond necklace. I looked up into the sky and saw shiny sequined stars around a slice of moon. I sighed at the beauty of the night and thought of Anna and Mina, wondering what they could see if they looked up at the sky right then.

    My nose steered me to the kitchen, where Aya and the cook were sitting at the table eating their dinner. I walked up to them and took a deep breath and said, "Can I have some?" Aya got up and fixed me a plate full of rice and dahl, while I pulled a chair to the table. There was a bowl of hot finger chilies and raw onion for a salad. Aya said that everyone had eaten, and Mummy told her to let me sleep. I was ravenous and dug into the food with my fingers like a "pukka Indian!" Cook and Aya thought I was so funny for making a simple meal sound like one fit for a king. I began to explain that I had not eaten anything so wonderful since I left for school, and I wouldn't care if they served this every day.

    Just then Mummy walked into the kitchen and put her

hand on my shoulder. "I see you have completely recovered," she said. I looked up at her smiling with my mouth full, nodding. She lovingly patted my head and told me that everyone was out on the promenade enjoying the cool night breeze, and I should join them when I was done with dinner. Mummy told Aya to bring out a large jug of lemonade for everyone, and then she and the cook could leave for the night. Mummy returned to the promenade while I stayed to finish my meal. Aya got up and fixed the lemonade, and the cook cleaned up the dishes.

We walked down the path to the promenade. Aya left the lemonade with Mummy, saying good night to everyone, and went back to the house. I was introduced to Roda's parents as "Mummy's little girl." I was quite shy, so I didn't linger with them too long; also, Roda was tugging at my dress to join her in hopscotch. There was plenty of light to see the big squares she had drawn in chalk, and now, with a full stomach, I started hopping. Roda and I became fast friends. She promised to teach me how to fly a kite the next day and wondered if I knew how to climb trees. I told her she had no idea that she was talking to a tree-climbing expert, which made us giggle and laugh through the evening. We planned all kinds of amazing things to do before Christmas, which was approximately three weeks away, and that night I went to bed quite happy and content.

It was late morning when I awoke to shouts of my name. I heard Aya tell Roda that I was still sleeping, and her response was, "Still?" I jumped out of bed and ran to the door and went out to greet her. Roda came back into the house with me and put her kite on my bed while she waited for me to hurry and clean up. I told her I had not eaten breakfast and asked if she wanted to have some too. She shook her head to say no while rubbing her tummy. She had already eaten a big breakfast.

 She sat with me in the kitchen while Aya served me toast and scrambled eggs with a big glass of milk. "Wow!" I said, getting laughs from Roda and Aya. I explained that I felt like the rich girls in school who ate this for breakfast every day out of real china plates just like the one I had. Roda and Aya gave each other quizzical looks and asked what I meant. I briefly told them about the meals served at school and how thankful I was to experience it here in my own home. Aya tousled my hair, but Roda, on the other hand, became gloomy. She wanted to know what it was like in boarding school and started asking me so many questions. I told her I wanted to go kite flying, but first I wanted to finish this wonderful breakfast. Then I would fill her in on Mother Doris.

 We went out to the promenade for my first lesson in kite flying. Roda showed me how to hold the sides gently and walk backward. She held a large wooden spool of string, unrolling as I walked backward to as far as she wanted. She yelled, "Stop!" so I did. Still yelling and making gestures with her arms to let go, she pulled on the string and the kite took flight. With a wondrous rush, the kite grabbed the wind, pulling its beautiful, long tail up into the sky. I ran back to where Roda stood controlling the kite's eager attempts to free itself from her grip, and she handed it to me. What a thrill I got when I realized I was on the other end of that frantically swaying kite. I kept screaming that it was going to fall into the sea, but Roda would just tug on the string, and it would listen to her. I learned to tug the string every time the kite tried to dive, and it would straighten out and steady itself. We must have unwound the whole reel, because the kite became so tiny up there, no bigger than a small bird. While we sat on the promenade wall dangling our feet over the beach, Roda and I took turns holding the kite as she explained how the boys would try and cut our kites to steal them.

"How?" I asked.

"With glass glued to their string," she replied. I asked how they accomplished this without cutting their hands. "Oh, that's easy. I've seen them do it. Want to try it?" she asked. I agreed.

Roda and I went to find Aya's son, Timothy. He was the expert in glassing kite string. Timothy was a skinny boy of about eleven. He was sitting outside his little shack smashing open almond pods when we approached with kite in hand.

"What you want?" he asked while stuffing the raw almond pieces into his mouth. Roda told him how we knew he was so clever at putting glass on kite string and wondered if he could help us do the same. Timothy laughed at us, saying, "Girls don't have kite fights. They are only good for flying them, while we come and cut them!"

"Please" we begged.

He got up and went into his shack and came out with a box of stuff. Sitting on the ground, he laid out his tools. He had a smooth stone for smashing broken bottle glass and a bowl of gook that looked like mashed-up rice. He told Roda to cut the kite off, and I was to hold the wooden handles of the wheel of string. He rolled up a wad of newspaper and started rolling string off the wheel. He said this was very dangerous and that we must never touch the first ten feet of string, closest to the kite. We both nodded in agreement and watched him continue rolling the first ten feet of string. Now we put everything down and sat with him on the ground to see the next process.

We watched in amazement how he carefully smashed the glass into small pieces that eventually turned into a fine powder. He put some water in the bowl of mashed rice and started mixing till it was smooth as paste and then dumped the powdered glass into it. He stirred it a couple of times with a stick, and then tucking one end of the wooden wheel under his arm he held the string out in front of him with his other hand. He grabbed a leaf from the ground and dipped it into the glass rice. Then he applied it to the string while rolling it up to reach the end.

Finally he had come to the last two feet of string and stopped. He said that we shouldn't put glass all the way up. Otherwise, we couldn't touch the string to attach a new kite if that one should get cut or destroyed. We just agreed with everything he said and thanked him for his help. We promised we would never try to cut his kite for all his help, but he only laughed, saying, "I won't promise nothing. If I want to cut yours, I will." He then gestured to us to follow him into his shack, which we did.

The room was dark, and it took a while for my eyes to adjust to see just how drab and poor the place was. Timothy showed us his area of the room, which he had decorated with a picture of Jesus, a makeshift altar, and a candle under it. Next to his mat on the floor he had a collection of kites. He pointed to his trophies won in kite fights, maybe just to scare us, we thought. He said he would be willing to sell us a kite if we ever lost ours and not to mess with him when he was out hunting. It all sounded so exciting that we begged him to let us watch the next time he was going to do it. I guess he loved the attention we gave him, and so he finally agreed.

I had to cringe at the way his room looked. The whole family shared that one room. Their kitchen was a coal stove outside the hut, and I kept thinking how lucky I was to have such a beautiful home. Even the boarding school was a zillion times better than what Timothy was living in. I see now what Anna said: "What you don't have, you can't miss." I felt Anna standing behind me shaking her head and giving me the all-knowing look. "Be thankful at all times!" I wished I could make it better for them, but then Anna also said, "We must want something bad enough to go after it ourselves; otherwise, when it is given to us, it is not appreciated." I guess when Timothy gets older he will go after his goals and achieve better, appreciating where he had come from on his way to his next destination. We left his hut with Timothy's words trailing: "Don't touch the glass part of the string."

What an exciting day I had. It was getting late, with lunch forgotten, so we ran home to wash up for dinner. I told Roda how I had missed my first sunset home and just had to be on the promenade to watch it that night. She ran home, promising to meet me down there, as she had never really noticed it the way I described it to her. I was washed and fed and out the door in less than an hour, just in time to watch the big red ball descend to the horizon. Roda joined me a few minutes later, and there we sat staring into the sun. I told her that if she held her breath and made a wish until the whole sun went under, her wish would come true. We both looked at each other, took a deep breath, and then I wished I would never have to leave home again and that Roda would always be here as my friend. I was running out of breath and looked at Roda, who had her cheeks puffed up as big as mine. The sun left a red glow over the horizon as we finally let the air out of our mouths to breathe again.

"What did you wish for, Tess?" she asked, and I told her. She laughed and said she had wished for the same thing. This meant that it was a double wish, and it would definitely come true. We finally gave up the day and went to our respective homes hoping to see each other tomorrow. But tomorrow never came.

***

"Hey, Tony. When did you get home?" I asked, and everyone turned to see our handsome soldier sitting behind us and listening to the story. "Daddy!" Vicky cried out and threw herself into his arms. Nick walked up to him like a big man and gave him a high five. Of course, Becky got her kiss and snuggles in, and then Tony bent over and kissed me on my head, saying, "Cool book you were reading. Did I miss a lot?" We all laughed and explained that it wasn't a book but shared memories.

"Wow, Tess. You should put it in a book," said Tony. "From the little I heard, I think it would make a great book!"

Becky said, "Definitely," with Vicky and Nick nodding their approval.

"A book sounds awesome, Becky, but what would the title be?" Vicky came up with *Jesus and Me*, or *Bad Nun*, but Nick said we should call it *The Adventures of Tess*.

It was getting late. I had work the next day, so I finally stood up and got my hugs in with Nick and Vicky asking when they would hear more. Becky, now standing with her arm around Tony, said, "We will get together on another weekend and finish the rest of the story. Tony will wait for the book, right?" as she tickled his sides. "Seriously, Mom, think about a title. It's really good and should be shared with others." Heading home, I wondered if it could really be a book. "Well, Jesus," I spoke out aloud in my silent car, "what do you think?"

Becky called me a week later to say that she would be in my area and we should do lunch. She wanted to hear about the part in my story that was not suitable for the kids. "How about we pick up some take-out and eat at my apartment?" I asked.

"It's a date, mom," she replied and said she would pick up food and bring it to my apartment that weekend.

"The kids have been asking about your next visit, as they are so into the story mom. How about next weekend? I thought about it and told her that she would have to prepare them for the next part by telling them that something awful happens to me, which will explain my change of attitude and behavior in the rest of my story. "First tell me what happened, and I will figure out what to tell them," she said. So, I began to tell her how things changed that third morning home for the holidays.

Stolen Innocence
Chapter 6

I awoke to shouts of "Oh, no! It can't be happening to me." I sat up in bed and looked over at Ava, who was looking in the mirror at the dresser.

"What's wrong?" I asked.

She turned around, and I got the shock of my life. She was covered in spots. "Mummy, Mummy," I screamed through the house, trying to find her. Aya and Mummy were doing the house accounts when I found them. I told her that Ava had big red spots all over her face, and I thought she was going to die! Mummy looked worried enough to run back with me.

I was looking at her face when Mummy came into the room. She pulled me away and told me not to touch anything. Ava had the measles, and it was very contagious. It was too close to Christmas for us to get sick, so I had to stay away for at least a week. "What do you mean, stay away Mummy?" I asked, following her out of the room. I heard her tell the doctor that her other daughter would spend a week at her cousin's house till the danger of contagion had passed.

"Which cousin? Who is my cousin?" I was starting to panic, and I just ran to Aya and started crying.

Aya held me in her arms while I told her I didn't want to go anywhere. I wanted to stay home. Mummy came into the kitchen and pried me away from Aya to explain, "Tess, you will love your cousin Erick. He is my favorite nephew, who would love to have you stay with them, just for a week, until Ava gets better. He has a beautiful wife, Elaine, and the cutest little baby about one year old named Johnny. Mr. Singh has offered to drive you to them, as I have to wait for the doctor to arrive. The sooner you leave, the safer you'll be. The week will just fly by, and we'll have a wonderful Christmas together." Aya packed a little suitcase for me, and I was out the door before I even had a chance to tell Roda what had happened.

I sat in silence all the way to Cousin Erick's apartment. I stared out the window of Mr. Singh's car, so angry that I was missing all the wonderful times Roda and I had planned. I was so looking forward to cutting someone's kite that day. I thought how unfair it was for Ava to do this to me. Why couldn't it have been her to leave instead of me? I guess that would not have worked out, since Mummy explained how contagious she was.

We had arrived at the apartment building. I stood on the curb and looked up but couldn't see the top. We must be in a different type of neighborhood, because there were no parks or open spaces to see the ocean. As far as the eye could see there were tall buildings and lots of traffic noise. I hated it already, and I hadn't even met them yet. Mr. Singh had my little suitcase and told me to follow him. We started climbing stairs, as the elevator was being repaired. Up and up we went until we reached the eighth floor. "We're here," he said and handed me my suitcase. He knocked on the door, and it was opened up immediately, as though someone was standing right behind it waiting for us.

"Hello, you must be Tess. Come in, Mr. Singh. Come in." Elaine was very pretty and sounded so sweet that I decided I would like her. Mr. Singh sat for a few minutes explaining the problem and then left.

Here I was, alone with strangers and wondering, What

now? Elaine picked up my suitcase and opened a door. She put her finger to her mouth to say, "Quiet," and called me to the door to see little Johnny fast asleep in the middle of this huge bed. It looked like two big beds pushed together to make one. He looked so cute curled up on his side with a little stuffed monkey clutched tightly under his arm. I smiled and couldn't wait to see him awake to play with him.

I was given a mixture of breakfast and lunch, which Elaine called "brunch," with a glass of orange juice. I learned that Erick would be home at six that evening, when he would be taking all of us to spend time with some of their friends at a private club. How thrilling that sounded. I wished Roda could have been with me to experience the adventure too. I had never been to a private club, whatever that was. Johnny woke up crying, and Elaine went into the room talking baby talk. When I entered the room, he had the biggest smile on his face and kept struggling to see me through his legs as his mummy tried to change his diaper. He blew spit bubbles at me and giggled, and I just fell in love with him. Elaine said it would be alright for me to climb in with him and play. That is where I was going to sleep too, right next to Johnny.

Erick came into the room saying, "Hello, hello, what have we here?" I turned to see this big man with wavy black hair and bright blue sparkling eyes, and a great big smile. He grabbed Johnny into his arms and threw him up into the air. Johnny squealed with joy as he kept doing it. Then he handed Johnny to a smiling Elaine and grabbed me by the waist and lifted me up to the ceiling. I thought I was going to go crashing through the roof at the speed I went up and then down again. He was such a tall man and so strong to be able to lift a ten year old like a rag doll. He hugged and kissed me on the cheeks and said he was so happy that I could spend time with them.

How could I not want to be there? They were so sweet and loving to me that I felt ashamed for doubting Mummy about them. I guess Roda could wait a week to catch up on climbing trees and kite fights.

The country club turned out to be a secluded home of a very rich person. He was so rich that he turned his estate into a yacht club. Cousin Erick was his closest friend, and I felt quite privileged getting special attention from all his other friends there. There was a private beach and swimming pool. The pool was actually part of the ocean but had walls built on three sides with the fourth open to the sea. There was a safety rope to represent the fourth wall in case inexperienced swimmers got swept out to sea.

Since there weren't any children there that evening I explored the grounds and the beachfront by myself. I stood in the water up to my ankles, allowing my feet to sink into the sand with each frothy little wave. It was pretty out there but too boring for a kid with nothing to do. I dried off my feet on the cool grass as I walked up to the main house, putting on my shoes at the front door. Inside, some were seated at a large round table playing cards, while others just sat around talking. Johnny was asleep on a deep couch, and Elaine gestured by patting the couch next to her to sit with her.

On the way home Erick sat in front with Elaine. It was the first time I saw a woman driving, as I thought only men were supposed to. Erick seemed very tired and leaned his head on the window, holding Johnny on his lap. In fact, they both seemed to be fast asleep. I had the whole back seat to myself, so I lay down and looked at the night sky. Erick woke up as we reached the apartment, and he carried Johnny up the stairs while Elaine held my hand to help me make it up eight flights of stairs. I was worried about Erick, though. He kept swaying from side to side, and I thought he might drop Johnny. Elaine didn't seem to worry, so I just followed behind.

I was helped into my blue clown pajamas that had funny faces all over. Some had large red noses, while others had smiling faces. Yet other wore frowns. Erick sat in the living room having a nightcap; that's what he called it. I asked Elaine if he had to wear it on his head, but she just laughed and explained that it was a drink of some kind that he had before bed. She pushed me over the bed rail to make the distance into bed shorter, and I crawled next to a sleeping Johnny and was out like a light.

I felt I was being suffocated! I opened my eyes to see Erick's big face near mine. He was breathing right into my mouth and touching my lips with his. The smell of his nightcap made me so sick that I wanted to puke. I couldn't understand what he was doing. I pulled my head away fast and turned to see if Elaine would explain what was going on. I saw for a split second that she was on the other side of the bed, so far away, and had her back toward me. I was about to call out when Erick put his big hand on my mouth and turned my face back to his. He leaned up on one elbow and with his other hand pulled my whole body up against his. I was very scared now and could not move. I thought he had gone mad and was going to kill me. He put his mouth on mine again, and he held my head so tight that I could not even wiggle free. He used his heavy body to hold mine down, still covering my mouth with his. He used his other hand to get into my pajama pants, stretching my legs apart. I pushed his hand away with all my might but couldn't budge it. He was so strong. I tried to hold my legs tightly shut, but all he did was hurt me with his big fingers in pushing them apart again. My stomach was hurting so bad that I knew I was going to die that night.

"Oh, please don't!" I screamed inside my head. He started moving his fingers in my private parts and stuck them into places I didn't even know I had! He dropped my head onto the pillow, finally letting me breathe, but he didn't stop with my body. I closed my eyes and thought I had to get up and run away fast. I thought, Why is this happening to me? What did I do to make him do this? What would Elaine think if she woke up and saw Erick touching me in my private parts? I had to force myself to move.

I remembered the girls on the train when they had to run to the bookstand and back. Ready, set, and go! I pulled away from his hand, which felt as though I was being ripped apart. "Hurry, hurry," I repeated in my mind as I dashed over the bed rail and ran to the bathroom. I stood there, pushing on the door from the inside even though I had locked it, wondering if he had followed me there. My ear was at the door to listen for any sound, but all I heard was my heart beating. I stayed at the door until I had calmed my heart and felt sure no one was approaching.

I held the door with one hand while I turned on the light. I looked at myself in the mirror over the sink, but it wasn't me. The face that looked back was so ugly. Her wet hair was stuck to her face in a grotesque way. Her lips were swollen to twice the normal size, and her eyes were red from the tears that were now gushing forth, leaving nothing of the face she remembered.

    I finally let go of the door and went closer to the mirror. I moved the hair away from my face and carefully touched my numb lips. I looked into my eyes and saw this horrid, angry, and very scared little girl. All I could think was, "What have you done?" I wanted to smash the mirror so I'd never have to look at her again. I looked around and saw the bathtub. I went to the door and listened. Not a sound. I opened the door and peeked around the room. No one was in sight. I stepped outside, tiptoeing to the bedroom.

    The bathroom light made the other rooms visible, allowing me to notice the three figures on the bed. Elaine had turned toward Erick, with her arm over little Johnny. He, on the other hand, was on his back with one arm across his chest and the other over my pillow. I wondered if anything really happened. It looked so normal with the three of them lying there. I went back to the bathroom and locked it once more. This time I didn't look in the mirror. I turned on the water to gently drip and plugged it with the stopper. My pajamas smelled so nasty, and the clown faces seemed to be laughing at me. I tore them off and sat in the filling tub. The water was cold, but it felt so good to my burning flesh. I must have sat in the tub for quite a while when I noticed little drops of blood floating back and forth on the bottom. I reached out and touched them, but they moved away from my finger and seemed to melt, blending into the water. *Maybe if I scrub real hard, all that had happened would come off; it might also erase my memory of earlier tonight.*

    My insides felt like they were on fire. I felt so alone that I started crying again, yet making sure not to make a sound. My thoughts drifted to Anna. *I wonder what she would say if I told her. She would probably never love me again if I did, and what about Jesus at Communion? How could He have let this happen, especially when He said He would always be with me. I should have said my prayers before going to bed, and maybe He would have stayed with me to protect me. It's all my fault for not thinking of Him, so that's why He left me alone to let this happen. I could never tell Mummy. She would be so angry with me for messing up this wonderful family that she loved.* I realized that I could never tell anyone. I don't know what I had done, but it sure made me feel so bad.

I splashed upright with fright when there was a knock on the door. I thought, "Oh, God, please don't let it be him. I don't want him to touch me again. Please, God." I was on my knees in the tub with my hand on my mouth so as not to make a sound. Elaine called my name and asked if I was going to be much longer. I took a couple of deep breaths and said, "I'm finished." I pulled up the plug to let the water drain and wrapped myself in a towel. I poked my head out the door and saw Elaine standing there holding Johnny. I asked her if she could please hand me some clean clothes from my suitcase, and she smiled and walked out of the room.

I shut the door and again pressed my ear to the door. I heard her coming back and unlocked the door once more. She placed my clothes on a chair outside the bathroom and told me I could dress there while she cleaned up Johnny. I told her I didn't want to dress in the open, but Elaine told me that there was no one else in the apartment but the baby and us girls. Erick had left for work hours ago. I must have spent the whole night in the tub, and now it was already morning.

I started to dress quickly, still watching the doorway, just in case he came back. I crept around the apartment checking all the rooms, making sure we were really alone.

When I was satisfied, I was able to breathe normally and sat on the couch to plan what to do next. I knew I had to get out of there fast before he came home that evening, but what could I do?

I sat at the dining table waiting for Elaine while my mind raced with confused thoughts of what had happened that night. Should I say something to her?

"I see you are ready for breakfast," she said as she came into the room. I jumped out of my seat and turned to see her with Johnny. She was still wiping his wet hair, and he giggled through an opening in the towel. He looked so cute that I couldn't help smile. How I wished I were a little baby with no fears and a loving mother to hold me.

Without really thinking out a plan, I mentioned to Elaine that I really missed Mummy and wanted to go home. "Aren't you having a good time here? Erick and I have so many fun things planned for you," she said.

"You are so nice, Elaine, but I really want to go home now, if possible." She explained that she would call Mummy so I could talk to her, but it wouldn't be possible for me to go home until Ava was over the infectious stages of the measles. She put Johnny into his high chair and started dialing the phone. The next thing I knew I was listening to Mummy yelling at me about how busy she was, that I was so ungrateful for the kindness shown by my cousins, and that I would be brought home on Sunday—and that was the soonest. She told me to put Elaine back on the phone, while I just slumped into my chair and cried.

Elaine was very kind and understanding, except she had no idea what I was feeling inside, and there was no way I could tell her. How I wished I were back in school with Anna.

I was stuck in a situation and didn't know how to get out of it. I spent most of the day standing on the balcony looking down at the busy street below. I wondered what it would feel like to float down to the pavement and get lost in the crowds. I sat in the lawn chair on the balcony and took short naps waking in fright every time I heard a noise.

Erick came out onto the balcony and rubbed my head. I jumped out of the chair, sending it toppling over. I darted past him into the living room and stood near Elaine. He wouldn't try anything if I was with her, I reasoned. Offering to help set the table for dinner, I totally ignored him. Elaine informed me that we were having company over—just my aunt Ella, Erick's mother, and her boyfriend. They come over once a week to play cards. I was quite relieved that there would be others around, and maybe he won't bother me tonight.

Aunty Ella was quite a character and seemed to know I was very troubled. She must have been watching me all evening. She had me sit next to her while she'd nudge me on which card to throw out, as though I knew what she was doing. I played along with her, which made me feel pretty comfortable. Aunty Ella asked Erick something about his first wife and his daughter my age, when suddenly Elaine remarked how late it was and told me to say good night and get to bed. I squirmed and made excuses that I wasn't tired and really didn't want to yet. Aunty Ella put her cards down and looked me in the eyes, asking, "Where are you sleeping, child?" Elaine answered for me and told her we all bunked together because there was plenty of room.

Aunt Ella stood up, shaking her head, saying, "Oh no, dear. Tess is a big girl and must have her own bed. She's probably uncomfortable in a big bed she's not used to. Where is the mattress that I usually use when I sleep over?" Elaine pointed to the closet. Aunty Ella pulled on the mattress that was stuck in the closet in a bent-over position, and then with a big tug it was set free. I jumped up to help carry it into the bedroom. I suggested that we could leave it out in the living room, but they voted against it. The only place left was on the same side where Erick slept. I watched them prepare the mattress with sheets and a pillow, pushing it toward the bed so the French doors to the balcony were not obstructed.

Aunty Ella finally said, "There, now you have your own bed," while hugging my shoulders and whispering, "Sweet dreams!" It's as if she knew!

I was left alone in the room while I changed my pillow to the far end of the mattress, and I lay down, still in my clothes, deciding not to change into my pajamas. Looking out the French doors up into the sky I could see the few scattered stars that shone with a special twinkle that brought peace to my soul. I wrapped my whole body in the sheet, resembling a cocoon with no visible openings up to my neck. I slept soundly that night, not waking once to any more disturbances.

The rest of the week passed fast, with Erick behaving as though nothing had happened, making me wonder if I had imagined the whole sordid ordeal. I must have experienced it because of the shame I felt whenever I was around them. I was so glad to be home that Sunday, even though Mummy pushed me to hug them good-bye when they dropped me off. I remember standing behind Mummy while they talked about my week and got slapped on the head by her for not showing enough manners in thanking them properly for the wonderful time they had shown me! How could Mummy have known what had happened? I could never tell her. I decided to keep it a secret until I was back at school, where I could either tell Anna or Father Anthony in confession.

    I ran through the halls as though I had only just arrived from school and suddenly remembered that Mummy never did explain why all of Daddy's paintings were gone. I found Ava in the living room, still covered in fading red spots. She actually smiled, showing she was glad I was back, and pointed to a large stack of comic books that our new friends had loaned her to read. I picked up a stack that she had already finished with and settled into the divan to read, but then I looked up and asked her if mummy had explained about the wall paintings. Ava nodded but kept reading. She said that it made Mummy so sad to be reminded of Daddy, so she had it painted over.

    I told her, "We had better not sing the song she wrote, either, if it's going to make her sad."

    "Too late. I already did," she said, not taking her eyes out of the comic book. Then, as if on cue, we gave each other a mischievous look and smiled. She turned out to be quite a pal that day, and I really felt happy to be home.

    The sunset and Roda that evening were very gratifying, and as much as I wanted to share my secret, I felt I could not find the right moment to do so. Roda seemed so childish with kites and tree climbing on her mind that I suddenly felt very old and dirty. I decided that I would not spoil her fun with awful thoughts. She pointed to the sun going down for the last second and held her breath to make a wish, while I just sat and watched how sweet her little heart was to still believe in it.

Christmas came and went with very little enthusiasm on my part. I had a dark secret that ate at my soul, and I just couldn't get into the festivities. We did the usual—singing carols around the piano, identical grotesque dresses made for Ava and myself, pictures taken with our friends, and, of course, midnight mass. The assembly was outdoors to accommodate the thousands that would not fit into the small church.

An altar was set up, with folding chairs stretching as far as the eye could see. Since I didn't like the candy apple red dress with big white squares that I was wearing and wished Anna could have made my Christmas dress instead, I sat between Mummy and Ava and tried to hide from snickering eyes. I hadn't been to confession; therefore, there was no way I was going to receive Communion. I didn't think Jesus liked me any longer, and I got angry with Him for not having protected me from that revolting incident. I decided not to trust Him any further, and I didn't believe He really existed. I had hardened my heart against God and felt that I had to take care of myself from now on, as no one else, not even God, could do the job.

When Ava and Mummy came back to their seats with Communion in their mouths, I thought how dense they looked with their eyes closed in prayer. And, for that matter, I become conscious of how stupid I must have looked when I believed that Jesus used to sit on my tooth and talk to me.

I found little interest in doing any more out-of-the-ordinary things, especially with it being our last week of the holidays. I just lay around the house reading comic books or occasionally joined Roda in her tree climbing exploits. I must admit it felt good perched high atop the mango tree able to see the ocean at my back and the main street in front. I could sit up there for hours without anyone noticing me, lost among the leaves and branches. I would wonder about the people on those buses and in their cars; did they have normal lives with places to go, people to see, or did they have nasty experiences like I did?

But what is normal, I thought. Roda seemed to have a different way of life. She didn't have to go away to a boarding school; in fact, a school bus would pick them up right at the house. They had plenty of money to buy beautiful clothes, maybe because they had a daddy that lived with them. I guess they were well protected by their parents and didn't have to rely on any God.

The horrid incident lingered in my mind, which made me wonder whenever I saw a man with a young child in tow if that little girl was also being molested. I worried for all kids, hoping they were all safe. The pain of remembering kept me aloof from Mummy and Ava, and I felt that being back at the convent would take care of the retribution I deserved.

I sat silently in the back seat of Mr. Singh's car while Mummy and Ava talked about school. Mummy was telling Ava that she had to make sure all the snacks that had been packed for us were equally shared. I gazed out the window watching life pass before I could focus on anyone or anything. Just when you think you recognize or accept something, it is past in a blink of an eye. I would not ever be able to savor the moment, enabling me to enjoy the good things happening in my life, because of the many bad changes. I just couldn't comprehend what was real and what was my imagination. I did make up my mind never to dwell on that day's events, as I knew that it too would pass, only to get buried deep within myself.

We were saying our good-byes and climbing into the train when I noticed the other girls gathered together showing mixed feelings, some in tears and others with smiles. They were sad to be leaving loving parents, yet happy to be reunited with friends. I also noticed that some of the girls were not there. *How lucky,* I thought. *They must have convinced their parents of the convent treatment and were kept back, probably to become day scholars close to home.* I overheard some say that their parents did not believe them because of the wonderful letters they had written all year.

I too had tried to tell Mummy that I didn't want to return. "Why can't we stay and become day scholars?" I asked Mummy. Mr. Singh spoke for her, saying, "Now, you know that school is a school wherever it is. You go there to learn, not to like it!" I looked at Mummy for her opinion, and when I didn't get one I went on to argue with him. I told him how badly the nuns treated us. I showed them my scars from whippings and how we are starved as punishment, and I even told them about the Mina incident and the box I was thrown into. Mummy stood up, and putting her arm around me, she said, "Now, you should know better than to tell lies about the good nuns, Tess. Out of the kindness of their hearts, they took you and Ava into that lovely school to give you a good education. You should be ashamed of yourself and ask Jesus to forgive you for saying such horrid things."

I was so desperate then that I asked Ava to corroborate what I had said. She had been listening to the conversation, but I guess when she realized that I was not believed, she added, "I can't wait to get back to school. I miss all my friends. It's going to be so great showing Mother Doris my paintings I did this holiday. Maybe she will help me enter it in the art competition." I was now totally ignored while Mummy and Mr. Singh started praising her, telling me that I should feel the same way too. It was a lost cause; my sister had turned on me once more. There it was again, people constantly letting me down. But as a so-called friend once said, "It, too, will pass!"

I had my head out the train window trying to blot out any conversations with the sound of the wheels drumming in my ears. Looking at the familiar sights, I noticed some foxes darting through the jungle bush. I stretched my neck out of the train to keep them in sight while I envied their freedom to roam. Foxes were so clever; Mother Doris could probably never catch one. I started imagining what it would look like with Mother Doris in her long white habit chasing the fox with her cane. The fox would stop and wag his tail at her, saying, "Catch me if you can! Ha!" I started smiling to myself and wished I were that fox. I'd give her a run she would never forget. The trip back to school seemed to end sooner than expected, and the whole group in our compartment spoke in hushed tones.

Pasco tried to cheer up the girls, who had turned very quiet on our way back to the convent. When the gates unlocked they all simultaneously started weeping. It was a frightening sight. This time I was not crying, just watching the others release their emotions. Even Ava had tears in her eyes. I was determined not to cry. I was going to be a fox and outsmart everyone. *I'll never let them hurt me ever again, but if they did, so what? I just won't feel it.* I jumped off the bus and ran toward the dormitory while the others just lingered around the bus. I first went looking for Mina, as I realized how much

I had missed her. I called out her name and ran through the little girls' dormitory and noticed a new face at Mina's bed. I ran out again and saw Mother Doris standing at the entrance. She had a big smile on her face, welcoming all of us back with open arms. She seemed different; she actually looked happy to see us.

I pushed through the crowd of girls and pulled on her skirt. "Where is Mina, Mother? I have looked all over and can't find her." Mother Doris put her arm on my shoulder and sadly told me that Mina had been adopted during the Christmas holidays to a very nice couple who wanted a child of their own. "No!" I screamed. "How could you give her away? How could you!" I started hitting and kicking her, not caring about the consequences.

I was so wrapped in my self-pity that I didn't realize the crowd of girls who were watching my arrogant behavior in horror. They were still all crying because they had to be there, and the spectacle I was causing put them over the edge. They started yelling and crying hysterically, with Mother Doris trying to hush them and control me at the same time. Mother Doris grabbed me by my waist and carried me, kicking and yelling, to her room while sternly telling the others to unpack and get settled in.

Mother Doris finally let go of me once we entered her room. I looked at her with such hate that she actually looked perturbed. She calmly sat down and motioned me to sit on her bed. I plopped myself on her bed while she pulled out her box of sweets and offered me one. I took it and just stuck it into my pocket, breathing very hard in anger. "Have you calmed down yet?" she asked.

"I don't know!" I replied angrily, which only made her

smile more. I couldn't understand why she was not beating me up instead of sitting there smiling. Mother Doris began explaining what happened to Mina, while I was made to feel very stupid over my behavior. It seems that Mina got very sick during the holidays. She developed pneumonia and was taken to the hospital. At that time, the nurse who took care of her fell in love with Mina and wanted to adopt her. When Mina pulled through, the nurse and her husband took her home to be their little girl. Mina was very happy with them, she told me, and said that I should be too. I looked up at Mother Doris not knowing what to say. I took the sweet out of my pocket and stuck it in my mouth. I guess the gesture explained that I had accepted her story and she was forgiven.

At least Mina had a family now who really wanted her, and I could be very happy for her, even though I would miss her so much. I wanted to go see Anna and be hugged by someone who cared. I had so much I wanted to tell her that I couldn't wait another moment.

"Now," said Mother Doris, "I will forgive you your behavior, but don't push your luck again. I will not tolerate such a scene again, understand?" I just nodded and walked out of her room and broke into a mad dash to see Anna.

Passing the girls with surprised faces that I had survived the wrath of Mother Doris, I somehow felt differently after that. I was now the big shot, not scared of anything or anyone. Yet, I couldn't help thinking, "It might pass!"

"Anna!" I yelled, banging on her door. The door opened, and I flew into her arms. Anna looked pale, and her hair wasn't combed. "What's wrong?" I asked. "Are you sick?" Anna just held me in her arms and hugged me without saying a word. My stomach started hurting, as I felt something dreadful coming. Anna walked me back into the room, explaining that her mother had passed away just before Christmas and she was exhausted from having cared for her before she died. She was so happy to have me back and wanted to know about my holiday. She said, "Don't leave anything out; tell me everything."

I told her how wonderful it was to see the ocean again and about my new friends, but I just couldn't bring myself to tell her about my cousin Erick. I wanted to, but I felt so ashamed, and I guess the ordeal showed on my face. Anna sensed there was something wrong and tried her best to dig it out of me. I finally told her that something bad happened to me during my holiday, but it was impossible for me to talk about it. Anna suggested that if it was bothering me so much I should talk to Father Anthony in confession, and maybe I could find peace in my heart. I laughed nervously and said, "I don't think so, Anna, because he is just a man and can't help me." Anna finally convinced me that he represented Christ, who hears all and forgives, and I shouldn't see him as just a man but a man of God. I thought I would give Christ another chance and confess this burden the next time I went to confession.

"Bless me, Father, for I have sinned," I said in the confessional. Father Anthony asked me how long it had been since my last confession, and I told him almost two months. I didn't know how to tell him what happened to me, but he helped by asking questions. I spilled out my heart to him and asked if there really was a God, and if so, would I be forgiven? Father Anthony took a deep breath and suggested that what had happened to me was very unfortunate, and he would pray for my soul and for God's forgiveness. He told me that I had to say a whole rosary for penance and never to talk of it again, especially to any of the other girls in school. My stomach hurt so badly by the time I left the confessional to say my penance that I was feeling worse than before. I had to say a whole rosary for penance, which was not good. I felt that I had committed such a heinous crime that even God would have to think about forgiving me. My heart was not in my prayer, as I still felt unclean. I stayed away from Anna as much as possible, because she always wanted to know if my problems were solved. I just shook my head, telling her that Father Anthony did not want me to talk about it to anyone, and I had to obey him if I wanted God to forgive me.

***

"Well, Becky, what do you think?"

"Poor Mom," she said. "You are very brave to have gone through all that alone. I understand now why you have been so protective of me while growing up. I think you can tell them about your exploits with Roda and even the part of going to your cousins' to get away from the measles; just don't say anything unusual happened. You can blame your change in attitude to being frustrated with your mom, who would not believe you.

"That may be so, but I do mention the sin I felt was my fault, and they will wonder what that was."

"Don't worry about it for the present; I will let you know what I tell the kids before you come to visit and finish the story."

"The next adventure is really awesome; it's called "the Great Escape," which I think you all will find very interesting

Were you serious that my stories should be a book?"

"Yes, of course, mom," she said. "I am still thinking of a title for you."

The Great Escape
Chapter 7

Ava was now in the big girl's dormitory. She turned thirteen in December. School would be starting up soon, and we all kept busy with books being covered, class schedules, and uniform fittings. While kneeling in front of my bed and struggling with a book cover, Mother Doris pulled me up to face her. She looked at me through angry eyes and told me to pack all my things and roll up my mattress. I looked at her in shock and asked why.

"Don't ask questions. Just do as you are told!" she said sternly. I felt terrible, because all the other girls were looking at me and also wondering why. I quickly did what she wanted and followed her into the big girl's dormitory. I got surprised looks from all of them too. Mother Doris pointed to a vacant bed and told me I was to stay there from now on, and I was not allowed to associate with either the little ones or the girls from my previous dormitory. I was so surprised that I could not find my voice to ask any questions.

Ava saw what was happening and came to Mother Doris, protesting, "She's only ten. She can't be in this dormitory. I had to wait till I was thirteen. It's not right," she kept insisting, thinking that I was privileged or something. Mother Doris just turned to her and coldly replied, "Take it up with Mother Superior. She told me to put Tess here." I threw all my things on the floor and darted past Mother Doris and Ava to find Mother Superior.

Mother Superior condoned what Father Anthony had done. "He was thinking of the many other souls that might be hurt by your sinful experience. It's best you stay with the big girls from now on." I was so humiliated knowing that Mother Superior knew about my sin, and now I was being banned to hell for it.

I was right. There is no God! How could Father Anthony have told my sin to Mother Superior? I thought that Father Anthony was supposed to keep it a secret between him, God, and me. I will never trust anyone ever again, not even Anna! I started to feel such a hate for everyone. I thought I could even kick a small baby if it tried to touch me. I wanted to die of shame. Everyone in school would know what a wicked and sinful girl I was. At this point I didn't care if anyone ever talked to me again.

***

"What sin, Nana? What happened to you?" said Nick, and I watched Vicky stick her fingers in her mouth, ready to bite her nails.

I looked at Becky for answers and was so glad when she simply told them that "Nana experienced something awful during her holidays and doesn't want to talk about it. Someday when you are older she will explain it all."

"OK," said Nick and Vicky in unison.

"May I continue with the story?" I asked.

"Please go on, Nana. This is getting very exciting," said Vicky.

***

I was treated like a leper from then on. I wasn't allowed to play with girls my own age and was pushed into a group of big girls who didn't want me around either. I started writing down all my memories, emotions, and hatred for the world, especially Jesus. My diary was now my only friend, and it listened to my heart without condemning me. After a few months of school I realized that my education meant nothing to me either. I failed every subject miserably and got severely punished for it. Mummy was informed of my bad grades, and I received pleading letters from her to do better in school.

Even Anna tried to reach me, but I decided not to love her anymore, so I hid from her attention. One day I confronted her with, "I don't trust anyone, not even you!" I told her not to pray for me, as I didn't believe there was a God. Anna saw the hatred in my eyes and wept. I wanted to run into her arms and hug her to apologize, but I stood firm and walked away.

I had turned eleven that year and was informed that mummy could not afford to have us home that Christmas, so we had to experience it in school that year. Ava was very unhappy, and I really didn't care. We realized how awful the girls who were left behind felt while we watched the rest of them climb aboard the school bus for the station and then home. We had both failed our grades and were required to be reexamined in order to get promoted. Even though it was the holidays, we still had study hall. Mother Doris would take Ava's math book and shove it into her face, screaming, "Study, study!"

After about a week of this treatment, Ava approached me with a scheme attached to a menacing smile. "We're going to run away, and you're going to help me," she told me. I wanted to but decided against it. I shook my head and told her that I didn't care about studying, and she could run away if she wanted without my help. I was still angry with her for not having stood by me when I tried to explain how horrid it was here in school. I remembered how she had let me down so many times before, and this was my chance to get even with her. I schemed in my own little head how I was going to let her get so far with her plans, and just when she thought she was going to make it I would tell Mother Doris of her plans. I'd see how she liked it! Ava turned in disgust from me and mumbled something and walked away.

I was grabbed by my ears and pulled to my locker. Mother Doris was pointing to the mess of peanut shells as she said, "I will not tolerate stealing in my school." I stared at the shells with a puzzled look. The peanuts were our Christmas present from the nuns, a large red stocking filled with roasted peanuts. I had been so angry at the stupid present that I gave my stocking away to another girl. I protested that I hadn't stolen any peanuts and that she, Mother Doris, had been a witness when I gave mine away. "I know," she said. "I guess you changed your mind and took them back." The girl I had given my peanuts to was standing next to Ava with head bent.

Ava spoke up now, "I told you not to take them, Tess. I would have given you some of mine if you wanted." She looked so pitiful that Mother Doris got even more angry, believing that I deliberately did this awful thing. Up went the cane, while the others backed off, giving her enough room to beat the tar out of me. With each stripe across my back she kept reminding me of how filled with sin I was with what I did last Christmas and now this. At the rate I was going, I was surely on my way to burn in hell. All my cries of innocence were in vain.

At lunch I was made to kneel at her refectory desk. "No lunch for you until you confess to stealing, the only way you can save your soul." I was given a chance to confess right there and be allowed to eat lunch. I refused! I had developed a stubborn streak and refused to confess to something I hadn't done. After lunch I was taken before Mother Superior. Alone with her, she tried kindness. "Now, Tess," she said, "you don't want to burn in hell, do you?" She waited for an answer, but I gave none. She went on, "All you have to do is confess it, and God will forgive you instantly."

I looked at her with hate and said, "If there is a God, why didn't He forgive me instantly when I confessed my other sin to Father Anthony?" Before I knew what happened, I was knocked to the floor with a slap across my face. Mother Superior was screaming at me for blaspheming God.

While still on the floor and holding my face, she kept repeating, "There is no hope for you in heaven; you now belong to the devil, and to hell with you. Get up and go to Mother Doris at once."

Mother Doris then took up the abuse and hit me around the head with her bunch of keys, telling me I was going to hell soon. I shielded my head with my arms and mumbled that I was already there. I was isolated from everyone and made to sit on the morning wash-up wall alone. I sat there burning with hate for everyone while my stomach ached for some food. I had not eaten since the night before, and now it was almost time for dinner.

I was feeling so faint from being beaten, the crying, and the loss of nourishment I thought it would be wonderful to just die that night. I didn't believe there was a hell because there wasn't a God, so where would I go? I imagined if I died that night I would become a ghost and haunt Mother Doris and the whole school forever, and I looked forward to scaring them to death.

Ava approached me while I sat alone. "Well? Have you had enough? I can stop it, you know. That is, if you decide to go with me. I can tell Mother Doris that the girl you gave the peanuts to made up the whole story." With no reaction from me, she slapped me on the head, saying, "It's up to you, stupid. Just think, we could still be home for Christmas." I finally nodded my agreement and gave in. I should have realized her power over me was even greater than any god!

I savored every morsel at breakfast while noticing Ava trying to get my attention. She had a look of excitement on her face that could have screamed to the world, "I'm out of here!" She managed to con Mother Doris's approval that I should help her study. While we sat there with open books she would start drawing maps. We were to escape that night. If I read her artistic clues correctly, she drew a black sky with the moon lighting the pathway we were going to take. A line of stick figure girls going down to the refectory with arrows pointing away from it toward the kitchen past the music cottage right to the closed gate. She drew a stick figure climbing the gate with another one running toward the train station. I whispered that those were tall gates with no ladders and only arrows. How were we going to get over them, especially in the dark? She smiled and nudged me in the ribs saying, "No problem." I guess she was more of a fox than I could ever dream to be.

This was it! Ava and I were last in line to the refectory that night. Just as we passed the nuns' refectory, she tugged my arm to fall back slowly. While the line started descending the steps, she and I made a mad dash toward the back gate. We hid near the well to make sure the coast was clear before we darted toward the bath stalls. It seemed like an eternity of holding our breath; it was time again to make another run to the music cottage and then freedom. We stepped out of hiding, ready to run the last stretch when we were stopped in our tracks, realizing that the dogs had been set loose to patrol the area. They were standing in front of the music cottage, their eyes glowing in the dark and slowly growling with rising pitch. While they readied themselves to pounce, we turned and ran as fast as we could back to the refectory.

Mother Doris was just about to start the prayer when we made it to our seats. Ava made the excuse that she had to stop and tie her shoelace, therefore making us late getting there. She looked very angry that her plan had misfired, but as she ate her dinner I would occasionally glance up at her to see that familiar smirk, which meant she had formulated another plan.

The next morning after breakfast chores were handed out. Ava volunteered my services to sweep up the long hallway, as well as the south balcony, while she would wash all the windows along the south side to keep an eye on me. Mother Doris was all smiles, surprised that she would have volunteered for anything, let alone a work detail. She handed us buckets, rags, and a broom, telling us to get to work. While my arms ached from pushing the broom, I kept thinking about the great escape. I realized that we had no supplies for the trip and started to doubt Ava's plan.

I had to have my diary with me, I thought. What if it fell into the wrong hands? I started thinking of excuses to leave my duty so I could retrieve my diary. I laid down the broom and ran toward the dormitory, finding Mother Doris sitting in a chair reading. She was in a place where she could overlook all the chores being done and immediately looked up as I approached. I hung my head as humbly as I could, explaining that I needed a large bag to collect trash while I swept. Mother Doris pointed to the bathroom and motioned to get one out of the supply closet. I ran to the back and grabbed a bag, then ran as fast as I could through all the dormitories to get to my bed. I grabbed my diary, put it into the bag, ran back to the bathroom, and then out again. Mother Doris had just gotten up from her chair and started walking in my direction; she wondered where I had gotten. I told her I had to use the bathroom and that I was going back to work. She kept walking to the back while I ran with my book and bag to resume sweeping.

I noticed Ava was also checking on my whereabouts, and I reassured her that everything was alright. I noticed the jambul tree was loaded with fruit, and a great bunch of them were lying on the ground. I loved jambul. They are the same size and shape as dates but not brown or wrinkled. Jambuls were sweet, purple, and always swollen with juice. The skin was so tender that a slight pinch would puncture it, squirting purple juice and easily staining clothing with a purple dye. I had grown accustomed to eating this fruit on many foodless days, and now I gathered them up into the bag. We had no money to buy food on the train, so we might as well have jambuls.

We were now at the south wall and close to the back gate. Ava spoke in whispers, saying, "It looks like the coast is clear. No one is watching. When I tell you to move to the gate, drop the broom near the bathroom and start climbing over. I will keep watch and then follow."

I nodded that I had understood and made my way toward the day scholar bathroom.

"Now!" she almost yelled.

I dropped the broom into the bathroom area and threw the bag over the gate. I was glad it had metal rungs and was easy to climb. I had barely dropped to the other side when she was over and running to the back of the school, yelling at me to keep up. We had the cover of the mango trees, but the wall in front of us seemed like an impossible task to undertake. The wall consisted of large guttered rocks with colored glass sticking out on top, plus another half foot of barbed wire.

We grabbed some of the mango tree branches and pulled ourselves almost to the brim of the wall, only to find there was no footing space without cutting open our hands and legs. Fortunately for me, I climbed more of the tree above the height of the wall, and from that vantage point I could see a clear path. I held my breath and jumped over the wall to freedom. Ava was still struggling with the wire and had blood dripping down her knees but didn't seem to care. She finally gave a loud yell while she threw herself over the side, ripping her dress.

We dusted ourselves off and started walking very casually across the street and then along the familiar path we had traveled to the train station. Every now and then she would realize her knees were stinging from the glass cuts and would pick up some discarded paper to wipe away the blood. Also, on occasion, we'd look behind us to see if we had been spotted, which usually brought our adrenaline flow directly to the feet, making us break into a fast run.

We had finally arrived and leaned against the station wall trying to catch our breath. Looking at each other's physical condition, we were a terrible mess needing some tidying up. We slipped into the restroom to clean up unobserved, but the attendant in there gave us curious looks. Ava immediately started a conversation with me for her benefit: "Hurry and wash up. Mummy will have a fit if we have to miss our train." The attendant got into the act of trying to help us hurry. She found a first-aid kit and bandaged her knee, wondering how she could have gotten so badly messed up. Ava said we had been waiting for quite a while for the train, and as sisters go, we had played rough, chasing each other around the station.

"What train are you waiting for" she asked.

"We are going to Bombay," replied Ava.

"You better hurry up, because the Bombay Special is pulling in right now," she said while pushing us out onto the platform. We looked quite respectable now and turned to thank her. I clutched the rolled-up sack and noticed the jambul juice had leaked onto my dress. I hid the stains with the bag, following her out to the platform. We had no tickets and looked so out of place: two little white girls on their own in a swarm of Indians, pushing and shoving each other to the front in order to catch the best compartment seat.

    Ava held on to my arm and managed to hide amongst the crowd. The train whistle could be heard, the bell at the station rang announcing the Bombay Special, and I was being suffocated, squashed up against some Indian woman. Suddenly, I felt an iron grip on my right arm. My bag now held to my chest, Ava was pulling on my left, while another hand pulled from the right.

    "Pasco!" I yelled, while my voice drowned in the sea of voices around me. Ava looked so desperate that she was prepared to get on the train with or without me. Being such a big man, Pasco was able to grab me by the waist with one hand while reaching for her with the other.

    "I told you it wouldn't work. It was a stupid idea. I don't know why I listen to you," she yelled at me. Pasco let go of her while he still had me in a vise-like grip. She grabbed one of my hands in order to show Pasco that she was helping him restrain me. I finally gave up and started crying hysterically. Pasco shook me by the shoulders while telling me I was in big trouble.

    The bus ride back to school is obscure, except for the vision of Ava sitting next to Pasco talking her way out of trouble. She blamed the whole episode as my foolish idea. She, being my older sister, could not let me run off by myself. I could have been hurt! I lay in the back of the bus with my feet up against the seat and buried my head of tears in my arms. I massaged my knees, knowing that I would be spending many hours on them and almost felt the pain before it had been dealt me.

Mother Superior stood in the doorway as we pulled up. Pasco waited for me to come to the front of the bus so he could hold me by the neck to deliver his captive. Ava was already with Mother Superior as I was dragged before the Inquisition. I figured, What was the use of trying to blame her? Who would believe me? I found Mother Doris inside the office and could not bring myself to look at her face.

Ava was dismissed to her pending chores while I was brought before the two nuns. First thing they did was to make me kneel in front of them while Mother Superior questioned me about the escape attempt. I took a deep breath and explained about the book being pushed into Ava's face, the peanut frame-up, the blackmail, the first attempt that failed, and then this one.

I closed my eyes and waited for the blows that were to follow my unbelievable story. Mother Doris was the first to speak. "It makes sense, Mother Superior; the child could not make up such a story." I straightened my hunched back and looked up at her in surprise. I wasn't sure I had heard right. Mother Doris and Mother Superior were standing with their backs to me, speaking in hushed tones.

Maybe there is a God, I thought, wondering what the outcome would be.

Mother Superior turned and motioned me to stand, saying, "You may go to your chores, Tess. Tell your sister I want to see her immediately."

I dusted off my sore knees, picked up my bag, and said I was sorry for all the trouble caused while I walked backward out of the office. I quickly got rid of the bag of jambuls, retrieved my diary, and changed my clothes. My diary was ruined; every page was juiced in purple and unreadable. I tossed it out too, knowing that I could write it again just from my memories.

Ava was sitting in study hall with her books up to her face pretending to study. I quietly walked up to her and put my finger on her book, pulling it down. She jumped in fright, but on seeing who it was she looked ready to slap the Dickens out of me. I quickly told her that she was wanted in the office, and I ran out of the study hall.

I watched her from a safe distance. She slowly dragged her feet, making her way to Mother Superior's office. I had to get closer to see the outcome. It was owed to me for a very long time. I inched my way along the wall, and once she had disappeared into the office I stooped under the open window to hear Mother Superior say, "Ava, I am very disappointed with you. I am afraid you have committed a tremendous—" Then it stopped. I kept waiting for her to continue. Instead, I heard Mother superior yell in panic, "Oh, God. Get the sick room nurse quickly." My sister, the brave bully, could not take the pressure and had fainted. I walked back to the dormitory thinking how lucky she was. She had beaten the system again. Someday she'd get her comeuppance, I hoped.

***

"Go on, Nana," said Vicky. "I think I have bitten off all my nails. This was so exciting but so scary. I wonder what would have happened if you both made it onto the train. Do you think your mom would have sent you back?"

"I don't know what she would have done, darling. All I know is that I never thought that far ahead. Life seemed to come at me so fast that all I could do was survive from day to day. It helped having my dear Anna to console and direct my steps, or I don't know how I would have turned out. I always remembered what Jesus told me: 'It will pass.'"

"Maybe that should be the title of your book, Nana," said Nick. "'It will pass.'"

"That's a good one, Nick. I'll keep it in mind."

"So, how did you escape from that awful place, Nana?" asked Vicky.

"Well, Vicky, I've saved the best for last!"

***

Eventually the nuns forgot my sin, and I was once again allowed into the company of girls my own age. I, too, had put it out of my mind and refused to think about it anymore. I was doing all right now, with hardly any beatings. I had reconciled with Anna, but somehow the distance between us remained. Many times I thought it was too good to be true, something had to happen to spoil my happiness soon. I found that as long as I was having fun, being happy, I had to balance it with some sort of self-punishment. I couldn't really be happy, anticipating a disaster every time I got that way, so I would sometimes go into a deep depression, isolating myself from my friends. I would go to confession and make up a bunch of sins for Father Anthony so he could play God and forgive me. I would be happy for a while with my friends, but then I would start the whole routine of punishing myself before Mother Doris could find a reason to whip me.

I was now receiving Holy Communion again at the urging of the nuns, but I would always swallow it before I got back to my pew. Somehow I was not ready to accept Jesus again, and I felt that if He really existed, not just in my imagination, He would find a way to talk to me. It was His turn to make first contact.

Also during that time I experienced another rite of passage. Once you reached thirteen, whether you needed it or not, you wore a bra. It was the rule! I put up a tremendous fight when Mother Doris and Ava tried to strap me into my first bra. I had such a flat chest that the brassiere cups just hung like deflated balloons. Mother Doris insisted that I keep it on until the bumps on my chest filled it in. A smile crossed Mother Doris's lips, and I laughed too. I had agreed to put one on, but only when the bumps started showing.

"Wear it!" she said in a determined way as I walked out of her room tossing the thing around my finger. The big girls giggled as Ava narrated the ordeal I had put her through. I walked up to one of them and asked if I could see what her bumps looked like so I could see how they fit in the contraption I was holding. She pulled away, yelling for Mother Doris. Being thirteen was to be a memorable year.

Free at Last
Chapter 8

After the last episode of running away, Ava had altogether given up studying. She had failed every class but got promoted anyway. With final exams around the corner she would doodle on all her books rather than open them.

During this time, we were given less playtime and more of study hall. On this particular evening we were told that Mother Doris had other business and was not available to sit with us. Instead, Mother Gina, an Italian nun with the rosiest cheeks—she could have passed for Mrs. Santa Claus if there were one—stood in the open doorway. She had a light mustache and looked like she weighed at least three hundred pounds with only five feet and a few inches to her height.

Mother Gina dropped her book satchel onto the desk with a loud thud, which got the attention of everyone in the room. "I will not have a single sound from any of you. I must have absolute quiet to grade the exam papers, and you are being warned now to ask any questions you may have before I sit down," she said. A few hands went up, and she dealt with their requests and then sat down.

Ava looked at me with a wicked smile and opened her desk. In there was her sewing kit, paints, and other craft materials. She quietly pulled out her scissors and pieces of cloth and started her project behind the cover of a book. She was such a talented artist that she could create anything she set her mind to. I went back to studying and occasionally looked her way to see if her project had developed any further. Out of the corner of my eye I noticed her movement when she would open and close her desk. I turned my head and saw the replica of Mother Gina in a six-inch doll. Ava was holding it up inside her desk and showing it to the girls around her, which in turn started a hushed giggle. I smiled at her genius and thought. What a wacky sister I had.

    Mother Gina looked up from her papers and searched the room with her eyes. Ava quickly shut the lid to her desk, but it was too late. Her mischief had been discovered. As usual, my stomach twisted with pain, and all I could think of was a way to protect her from harm. If Mother Gina discovered the doll, there is no telling what she would have done to her. I moved my elbow over my stack of books and started inching them to the edge. Mother Gina walked toward Ava and brought her ruler down on her hands with such a vicious blow that I thought I was going to see her fingers cut off.

    I pushed my books off the desk, and they landed with a loud bang, bringing Mother Gina's attention toward me. I bent down to pick up the books and glanced at Ava in concern. I hoped her hands were not damaged and that she would still be able to draw, paint, and play the piano.

    Wham! The ruler came down across my head, followed by my stack of books that she grabbed out of my hands. She slammed them into my bleeding scull, letting my books scatter all over the desk and floor. The girls around me started screaming at the sight of blood, but Mother Gina wanted more. Her hand went up with the ruler once more, but I intercepted it with my arm and then grabbed it out of her hand. I was so angry and incoherent that I couldn't think of what I was doing. I remember lashing out at her with the ruler and beating her silly. She was covered in my blood, or I had really done some damage to her. The screams in the room were at a high pitch, and all I can remember was throwing my books at her, screaming profanities. I ran out of the room, leaving a thunderstruck audience. My first single-handed revolt!

    My head throbbed as I raised my hand to it, and I felt a huge lump that had formed with blood trickling down my face. I could not cry earlier because I was so angry. Now I was scared and hurting so much that I just wanted to die. I found myself staggering aimlessly, crying hysterically. My sobs were coming through my guts in such groaning; it felt as though my spirit or soul had left me. I was an empty piece of flesh with no thoughts of past, present, or any future. I felt I might suffocate with this overwhelming feeling of loneliness if I didn't find a way out of there. I found myself running toward the front entrance gate, and to my utter surprise, no one was in pursuit. I hurled myself against the locked gate in hopes of breaking out, but it was locked tight. I grabbed a fist full of the iron bars and shook back and forth, when suddenly one side moved ever so slightly to the side. It made a small opening between the two halves. I stuck my head through the opening and then squeezed the rest of my body, inch by inch, until I finally pulled free. I was now on the outside looking in.

    A sudden rush of adrenaline jogged my memory, and I took off along the wall of the school into a large, open field. It seemed exceptionally dark that night, with only the moon and stars for light. I couldn't decide on what action to take, feeling at a complete loss because, once again, I had not planned ahead. I crawled under a hedge near the school wall trying to make sense of what just happened.

    I decided to stay close to the school grounds and

consider what to do in the morning. I pulled aside parts of the hedge to dig in for better cover when I noticed a broken section of stones that could, with some effort, be pushed through. I dug at the blocks for endless hours, it would seem, until I was able to free at least three, leaving a small opening for me to crawl through. I was now pulling myself through the hole and came face to face with the back of the dormitory bathroom. The smell was nauseating, but I didn't care. I lay on the grass and looked up at the flickering stars, thinking that if I should die that night no one would find me till the bathroom waste was removed, and that could be days. I pulled myself up and leaned against the wall and then decided to crawl back to the small opening, hoping that my head would stop pounding.

    I thought I was imagining it when I heard my name being called. No, there it was again: "Tess," a shout of many voices in unison. I knew I had really heard it this time, so I scrambled out of the opening I had made in the wall and poked my head through. I focused my eyes in the dark and was able to make out a line of white robes. They were holding hands and calling out my name. They were searching for me!

    I felt the lump on my head, which was now as big as a ping-pong ball, and the pain was unbearable. I almost wished they would find me; I didn't want to die yet. I could hear Ava's voice out there too. They were close now, and I overheard her crying, "It's all your fault that she ran away. You are all so cruel. If anything happens to her, I hope you all get put in jail. Tess, Tess," she cried out. My sister really cared about me. *She loves me*, I thought, with a warm feeling inside. I pushed through the opening again to call out to Ava, but the effort it took pulled me toward a black hole of darkness.

I opened my eyes to find my bed surrounded by nuns. They looked like the seven dwarfs discovering Snow White for the first time. I had barely focused on their faces when one of them took it upon herself to be judge and jury and slapped me into unconsciousness again.

When I awoke again, I kept my eyes closed listening for familiar sounds. I realized I was not in the dormitory anymore but in the infirmary with Anna caring for me. I refused to open my eyes just in case I'd get slapped around again, but something told me that I was going to be alright. Anna had a cold towel on my head while she rubbed her fingers over my forehead. She was talking very gently to me on how I had given everyone such a fright. It felt so good, but I dared not open my eyes yet. It was so much safer in the dark.

I heard Mother Gina's voice in the background. I also heard the nurse telling her that she had hurt me very seriously and that she should be more careful when punishing the children. I was also surprised to hear Mother Gina weep with apologies for her uncontrolled temper. She wished I would wake up so she could make amends. I felt a calm come over me, wanting so much to open my eyes. I thought against it. *What if it was a trick to get me to wake up just so they can put me out again?*

I waited till the room was quiet again and then very slowly squinted my eyes to look around. The room was empty, except for a lone figure standing at the window. I opened my eyes and called out to Anna.

"I have been praying to our Lord Jesus to bring you

back to me, Tess, and here you are." She smiled with tears running down her cheeks. She was rocking me in her arms as though I were a little baby. Even though my head still hurt, her arms around me were all the medicine I needed. Anna rushed out of the room and brought the nurse back with her.

While Anna spoon-fed me some soup, she told me what had happened that week. I was shocked to find that I had been in and out of consciousness for a whole week.

"Hey, little one," came a voice around the corner. I looked away from Anna to see Ava standing in the doorway. She had the biggest smile on her face as she approached me and knelt at my side. She looked at Anna, then at me, and popped her hand up from behind her back. I couldn't help but laugh, even though it hurt. She gave me the Gina doll that had caused the whole mess. How I loved my sister. She had finally let me into her heart.

"Next time let me fight my own battles, sis. I'm bigger than you," she said, laughing.

Anna just laughed and shook her head, saying, "You kids are unbelievable!" Anna finally told her to leave so I could get some rest and finished feeding me my soup.

I looked into dear Anna's worn face and thanked her for caring for me so much, even though I didn't deserve it. I told her how I had missed her these past two years, and I just felt so awful shutting her out. She just smiled and said, "I have been praying for you all this time, and I knew Jesus would bring you back, only I didn't know when."

"Is there really a God, Anna?" I asked. "Why do I doubt Him even though deep down I believe He exists? Why did He let all those horrible things happen to me? Why didn't He stop me from getting hurt?" I was crying because I felt so confused about God and wanted so much to understand Him.

Anna explained that God had a plan for each and every person He had created, and only He knew the answer. "We must have sufficient faith to believe that He is listening and talk to Him as though He were right here in person. We may not hear His voice through our ears, but we would feel it in our hearts."

I told Anna how I used to feel that way once, but that I stopped believing after that terrible Christmas when I was ten. Anna remembered how upset I had been, and she wondered if I could talk about it now. It was an old memory that brought back the horror and pain of that night. I held Anna's hand and through my tears told her the burden of my soul. Anna's hand tightened around mine as she cried with me, finally understanding how alone I was with a hurt no human could mend. She finally spoke such wonderful words of peace that I felt a weight lifted off my heart. "Tess, you are pure and white as the lilies of the field. It was not your sin to bear, but his. Satan is very clever; he knew that you belonged to Jesus, so he turned you against Him by stealing your heart and soul away from Him. Satan didn't like your precious relationship with God because he was jealous, causing all those awful things to happen, all the while expecting you to break away from God. Even though he is a priest, Father Anthony was wrong to talk about your confession. Remember, Tess, it was not your fault or your sin, and I am sure Jesus has longed to tell you that Himself if you'd only let Him."

It took me another two weeks in the infirmary, and I completely missed my final exams. In spite of it, I was promoted to the eighth standard. I learned that one of the rich girls who had witnessed my demise that night was rushed to a hospital with severe chest pains. Not only did she recover, but she was able to get in touch with most of the girls' families with the help of her parents.

Once I was released from the infirmary all the nuns treated us with delicate gloves. Mother Doris had mysteriously been transferred to another convent, and I never saw Mother Gina again. It was peaceful without the extreme discipline after that, and life in the convent was starting to look brighter. I guess God did speak to me after all by using me as a vessel to bring about this wonderful change. It was worth all the pain just to see the happy faces and the sweet nuns that replaced the sadistic ones.

I chose to believe that God did exist, but I just didn't understand Him completely. I would often pray, "Dear God, please let it stay peaceful like this with no more pain. But if I start to hurt again I'll know You know about it and will protect me. Please don't let me ever leave Your side again."

Approximately two months had passed since my injury, and life was wonderful. Even our meals had improved to a substantial amount with a variety of choices. Every Sunday the boarders would dress in their white uniforms, which had a blue-striped sailor's collar, and be taken for a long walk around the perimeter of the school on the outside! I would try to sneak to the back of the line so I could be close to Anna, who accompanied us, but even at thirteen I was considered a little undersized and had to be up front with the smaller kids.

On one of these outings as we had just turned into the main entrance gates we heard an awful screeching of tires and a loud bang, followed by horrific screams. The front of the line had already started down the pathway, but I broke free to run to the back. My stomach had not hurt like this in such a long time that the pain once again, I realized, was tearing at the false security I had developed. "Please God, please God, please God," I kept repeating out loud as I reached the end of the line.

  The nun who walked at the back was lying in a pool of blood, her white habit slowly turning red. The car that sideswiped the line was smashed against the convent wall, while the traumatized girls and a bunch of bystanders surrounded the fallen nun. I could hear the sound of the police sirens approaching as I pushed through the crowds looking for that familiar face I loved so much. "Please, God, let her be alright," I prayed over and over until I screamed. "Anna!" She was just barely caught between the car and the wall and seemed to be trying to push the car off all by herself. I screamed to the others to help get her out, but the crowds only got louder and bigger as the police approached. I grabbed Anna and told her I would not leave her alone and that help was on its way. Anna just smiled and tried to comfort me instead, reassuring me that she was fine. I looked at the crowds being dispersed, and finally the police reached Anna. It felt like an eternity that she was pinned to the wall, and now they pulled the man out of the car first. I started yelling at the police to help Anna first, but they were more concerned at arresting the drunken man who had caused the accident.

  The police officers looked me in the eyes while I screamed at him to move the car. He jumped behind the wheel and started the car, still looking into my angry eyes as he backed the car away from my precious Anna. He jumped out of the car and ran toward us just in time to catch her from falling forward. The police officer carried my smiling Anna to the waiting ambulance while I held onto her hand. I leaned over to kiss her good-bye when she whispered, "Don't blame God for this. I don't." Her voice trailed off as I was grabbed back by another nun. I wanted Anna to hear my answer, and I yelled back, "I won't, Anna. I promise."

    A week after the terrible accident there was a tremendous shake-up in the school. News of the hardships at school was basis enough for every parent to arrive and take their children home. Anna was recovering well in the hospital, and I even got to go visit her a couple of times. She told me she would stay on at the convent in order to care for the other children that God would place in her path. I told her how much I loved her and would carry her in my heart for the rest of my life. She could move in with Jesus, and we would always be together.

    I knew it would be a matter of days before I left St. Mary's for good to return to Bombay and a new school, but Ava and I were shocked to see Mummy walk into the dormitory. I almost fell over when she came running to me and held me in her arms, saying, "I'm so sorry, baby. I should have believed you." I hugged her back and told her it was alright now that she was here. Ava got her hugs too. Mummy had heard about the tragedy on the radio and called the school for details. Mother Superior told Mummy to come for us, as the convent would be closing the boarding school for a while. We packed in a hurry while Pasco loaded a real taxi with our trunks. I guess Mummy had already said her good-byes to the nuns, and we were off. I took one last look through the back window as we pulled out of the driveway. "Good-bye, Anna. Thank you, Jesus, for saving her," I whispered.

***

I had barely gotten home from my visit with the kids when my cell phone rang. It was an excited Becky saying she found the perfect title for the book. She said, "Are you sitting down?"

"I'm still driving, Becky. Of course I'm sitting down," I laughed.

She began telling me how she could not stop thinking about the story, and it finally came to her. "Here it is," she said. "The title for your book is *Zebra Tears*." I sat there in silence when she called out again, "Mom, did you hear me? *Zebra Tears!*"

"I heard you, baby. It is perfect!"

When I was a child, I spoke and thought and reasoned as a child. But when I grew up, I put away childish things. Now we see things imperfectly as in a cloudy mirror, but then we will see everything with perfect clarity. All that I know now is partial and incomplete, but then I will know everything completely, just as God knows me completely.

—1 Corinthians 13:11–12, NLT

About the Author

T. S. Vallée, known as Terri to family and friends, is a mother of two children and a grandmother to five, Nicholas, Victoria, Michael, Matthew, and Nathaniel. She has a jail ministry where she continually writes, encourages, and provides Christian books to inmates. Terri is the Sr. Customer Service agent at Charisma Media, located in Lake Mary, Florida.

Contact the author by emailing chp@charismamedia.com or write to:

T.S. Vallée
C/o CHP
600 Rinehart Road
Lake Mary, FL 32746

DEXTER DISTRICT LIBRARY
3255 ALPINE ST
DEXTER, MI 48130